A CLOSER LOOK

Pamela Fernandez

PAMELA FERNANDEZ

A Closer Look

Chapter 1

~~~

THE WEAK STREAM Of words struggled from her parched lips just as her spirit escaped her limp body. It went somewhere - while the shell of what once was her, remained.

"Nurse!"

The attending nurse came quickly and began to maneuver the stethoscope over the patient's chest searching for any sign of a beat from her heart. Then with compassionate authority the nurse softly announced, "She has passed."

Passed? Passed what- the test of life? Passed the finish line? No, nurse, her empty body lies here.

It's up to someone out there to determine if she has passed or failed.

The nurse left and Laven was alone looking down at the small lifeless form that had previously been her mother. Being alone was not new to her but she wondered what she was to do next. Cry? Those tears for not having a mother had been spent years ago. Her tear wells rested empty. Pain and sadness were present, but only because there would never be an opportunity for her mother to apologize. There would never be a chance for her to make things right.

Laven studied the hospital bed. It was cold and, despite the mechanical design efforts, uncomfortable. It was built to be temporary. Her mind drifted back to a stark white room made even more rigid with florescent lighting.

There were rows of similar, less comfortable beds lining opposing walls. One of those beds was hers.

It wasn't temporary. Laven had slept lonely in that

bed throughout her tender years. That bed had caught many little tears.

She pulled her attention back to the bed in front of her, holding what once had been her mother. She mused at how both the body and the bed were meant to be temporary. Her mother was gone but her final words seem to echo in the room.

Those important last words- were they to encourage me, or to tell me she loves me?

No!

When she numbly walked out, she found that those last words were not echoing in the room but rather bouncing in her cranial cavity taunting her into confusion.

Okay, I was unable to check the cry box off the list. What am I suppose to do next? There is no list, no one to ask.

She couldn't remember getting into the car, but it was moving on the road. She clinched the steering wheel. It felt as if the road was moving her like a treadmill. The car was in motion, but she had nowhere to go. As the wheels turned on the pavement, her mind was traveling over the parting words left by her mother.

Was this the last dose of hurt she would deal me, the final abandonment, a cruel joke? Did she dislike me so much that she would use her last ounce of strength to further injure me emotionally?

Just last week, she had asked me to come because she had something important to share with me. I had high hopes and seven days to build my expectations to mountain high peaks. And then...

The startling sound of screeching brakes made Laven instinctively brace herself.

Then came the jarring jolt and a crashing sound of metal against metal.

Laven's neck stretched causing her stud earring to dig into her shoulder and then whip back in the other direction. Her head struck something and blackness closed around her.

~

Voices mumbled and her eyes managed to open.

The light, the bright light that people who have returned from the grip of death describe. It's there!

"Did I die, too?" she asked, afraid of the answer.

A shadow blocked the light and slowly a woman's face came into focus.

"No, dear, you are among the living."

Laven tried to focus on the face, afraid that she was supposed to know this stranger. "Where am I?"

"You are in the emergency room. Someone hit you. Your vitals are good. You are going to be fine. They said it was a nasty crash. Someone up there was watching over you."

Laven looked into the eyes of the pretty young nurse. They sparkled. Her hair was pulled back in a tight bun and she wore a name pin on her uniform that read, "Libby."

Nurse Libby was busy reading a beeping machine next to Laven. A moment later, she turned and opened a plastic baggie.

The pretty nurse dangled the thin silver chain holding a small uniquely designed key and then placed it in Laven's hand. "Here is your necklace."

"Thank you." She said as she struggled uncomfortably to turn herself and put it back around her neck.

It was the last thing her mother had given her. She had no way of knowing what it unlocked, but she would make it her mission to find out. It could be the key that would open a lot of buried answers.

Now more aware of her situation, Laven began to panic. "I need to get out of here. I can't be in here." She was trying to pull herself up as she spoke.

The nice nurse, thinking Laven was in shock, tried to calm her nerves. "Okay, lie still until the doctor returns. Everything will be fine."

Laven shook her off and tried to sit up. "No, you don't understand! I have to get out of here. Please!"

The nurse put her paperwork down and took Laven's hand. I'm sure the doctor will be in soon." Nurse Libby sat down, making direct contact with her light blue eyes. "Sweetheart, you are safe here. You have my word." She smiled reassuringly, and oddly, Laven believed her.

"Why do you hate hospitals so much? Has someone tried to hurt you?"

Laven drew in a deep breath. "Trust me, I have my reasons, but if I told you, it would mean having to stay here longer and that I don't want to do."

The nurse studied Laven's face. "Does it have something to do with the person who hit your car? Was it someone you knew? Can I help you?"

Laven shook her head, surprised when it made her feel a bit dizzy. "No, nothing like that. As a child there were incidents that were very traumatizing to me. This place brings all those memories back. I just really want to go."

The nurse saw the fear etched in Laven's eyes and handed her a glass of water. "You are afraid of hospitals after a bad childhood stay. It's alright, most people don't love hospitals."

She smiled a bright smile at Laven. "They even have to pay me to stay here." The nurse stood and brought a cool cloth for Laven's face. "Try to relax and I will see what I can do."

Laven did try to relax. They would never let her leave if they thought she was having a panic attack.

She took deep breaths and tried desperately to think happy thoughts.

The door opened a few minutes later. It wasn't the doctor who entered, but two policemen bringing with them lots of questions. There was another time with other policemen. Back then; her answers to their inquiries seemed to fall flat.

Her mind wandered back in time. Sally was the meanest girl in the orphanage and as a result no one liked her.

The girls played off of her last name, Rue, and called her Rude behind her back. That's why it was hard to understand how she could convince them to follow her in bullying Laven. There was a hate for Laven in her heart that only seemed to grow. No matter how nice Laven treated her or how many gifts she gave to her, the bullying only worsened.

As luck, or better yet, un-luck would have it; they ended up in the same foster house. They weren't little any longer and that hate had grown even faster than they had. Four teenagers were crammed into a small bedroom. Sally spent her spare time playing hurtful tricks targeted only at Laven. Here, her nickname had grown more sophisticated. They referred to Sally Ella as salmonella, but behind her back they just called her Poison.

That dark night, the name couldn't have been more fitting.

She raided the foster parent's medicine cabinet,

crushed up the prescribed pills and placed the narcotic powder in Laven's glass, and then called for a chugging contest to see who could be first to finish their Pepsi. Laven had won the contest but nearly lost her life.

Sally screamed with feigned fear that Laven had attempted suicide as the medics rushed her out to the ambulance.

After pumping her stomach, they secured her arms and legs to the bed, citing it was for safety purposes to prevent her from harming herself

She had told the police her account of what happened. She would do the same tonight. She would do just about anything to get out of this place.

"Laven, do you feel like talking?"

"Yes. I was crossing the intersection and all at once I heard crashing metal and then everything went black."

"Had you been drinking?"

"No, I don't drink."

"That lines up with the eye witness report."

"Okay, then can I get out of here?"

"That's the doctor's call. Can you sign here?"

When the officers left, the nurse returned. Laven looked into her light blue eyes surrounded by long dark lashes. Anyone who could slick their hair so tightly that it practically lifted their eyebrows and could still be pretty, amazed Laven.

"Please! Can you get the doctor to release me?"

"Try to relax and I'll see if I can locate the doctor."

Just as she ended her plea for release, the doctor entered the room.

"Hi there, Miss," he looked at her chart and added, "Miss Hoddy. Everything looks good.

You can be discharged with the signature of a responsible adult to keep you under observation for 24 hours." He wrote something and went to the next patient.

"Please, Libby. Help me get out of here."

"Do you have someone who can stay with you while you recuperate?"

"I don't know anyone here, but I will find someone to stay with me. Just let me out of here. Where is my purse?"

"The doctor won't release you unless you have someone to watch you."

"Please!" Laven began to sweat in desperation.

"Look, I would be happy to stay with you, but I just started my shift.

Laven pulled herself up on the side of the bed.

"Wait. I know the guy that came in with you very well. He is a Christian. I can ask him to watch you until I get off after midnight."

"Came in with me?"

"Yes, he witnessed the accident and called the ambulance. He is out there in the waiting room."

"But... "

If you aren't comfortable with that, you can rest here until I get off. I know the doctor won't release you unless you have a responsible person with you."

No, No, I can't stay here."

"Shall I check to see if he will sign to observe you? Believe me he is a Christian."

Being a Christian wasn't necessarily a good thing for Laven, but if that was her only escape she would take it. She sighed and hesitantly agreed. Libby left the room and Laven contemplated a better escape. Where would she go? She needed her purse.

When Libby returned and wheeled her out to him, Laven wondered if she had made the right decision. There were two people seated in the waiting room. One had a magazine covering her face. The one Libby had spoken of was holding her purse.

A complete stranger is holding my purse!

The Doctor walked in and stood between the stranger and Laven. His tone was authoritative. "Be sure to watch for any disruption in the function of her brain. This could come in the form of headaches or dizziness. For the next few days, she should return if she experiences memory lapse, is dazed or confused, has nausea, or is off balance. Do you have any questions?" The stranger shook his head. "Call this number if any should come to mind." The Doctor extended his hand to end the conversation and seal the deal. If the Doctor had any reservations about this man, Laven was unable to detect them.

Moments and a stack of signed documents later, a complete stranger was holding Laven and helping her out of the wheelchair and into his unfortunate looking car.

As soon as the nurse escort was back inside the hospital, Laven spoke her first words to the stranger. "Okay, thanks for your help. I'll call a cab and you can have your evening back."

"Nonsense, I signed a release promising to observe you for 24 hours. I have to admit this was without a doubt the most pleasant promise I have ever made." His grin looked genuine, but that didn't stop Laven.

"Really, this has been a very hard day for me.

I would rather be alone, so you can drop me off at .. "Laven dug a slip of paper out of her purse and read aloud,

"6336 Checquered Lane."

"I gave my word to observe you. A man's word is his oath. Could you eat something?"

This guy is nice but I suppose the majority of serial killers begin that way.

"No. Thanks... Well, maybe."

"How about we grab something to eat and then go to a movie. You need to stay awake to ensure you don't have a concussion. You can watch the movie and I will keep my oath and watch you."

"That would be kind of cold."

"Ha! Rising Falls may be a smaller town than you are accustomed to, but we do have indoor temperature controlled movie theaters."

She had to smile.

"Is it a plan then?"

"I don't think that would be on the 'to do' list on the day your mother died."

He looked shocked. "Your mother died today?"

"Well, sort of."

"Dying is quite a definite thing. Well, unless, of course, you are farm boy in the movie Princess Bride. Seriously, did she really die today?"

"She started dying, to me, a long time ago. Today she made it official."

"I am so sorry. I had no idea."

"I am sorry too. I am sad that she will never be able to make things right."

"What do you mean?"

"I don't want to talk about it."

"Sure, I understand. To say you've had a bad day would turn most bad days into a holiday. I know a really good restaurant. Let's go."

His kindness felt awkward.

I am no stranger to being alone but tonight I am alone with a stranger.

"Please excuse my new car."

"New?"

"New to me. I haven't had a chance to clean it yet. I just traded for it."

Laven glanced around the shabby interior. It was brutally worn and diminished of any value. She wondered what he had traded for it, a moped, an old pair of shoes?

Keeping her thoughts concealed and with a comforting smile she uttered, "It's just fine."

His soft returning smile revealed his satisfaction with her response.

Poor guy...very, very poor guy.

"Is there a seat belt law in this state?"

"Yes, I believe that one is universal."

"Well, I'll hold it in place then. The little clasp thing seems to be elsewhere."

"Opps! I'll add that to the fix-it list. Would you feel safer in the back seat?"

"No, I'm good."

"After someone slamming into you, I know you must be jumpy. I will drive defensively and pray for protection."

Jumpy, not so much. Nervous riding with him, yes! She wondered if she should be the one calling out for protection.

~

"That is an unusual key. Does it fit a lock or is it merely ornamental?

"I'm not sure, but I plan to find out. I am hoping it opens up a box of answers."

"Interesting. You aren't eating very much. Do you want to order something different?"

"No, food doesn't go down well when you are being stared at."

"Sorry, I gave my oath to watch you."

"Aren't you going a little overboard with this?"

"Not at all. Part of it is the oath I signed, but you are a beatific vision."

"Dare I ask what that is?"

If a smile can shine, his did. "The sight of you is holy bliss to my eyes."

"Come on!"

"I can't help myself. You are very pretty."

Laven pressed hard into the back of her seat hoping it would swallow her.

This has gone beyond awkward. I wish I could disappear. If he really saw me, the real me, he wouldn't think I was pretty. I can't let him see the real me. If he did, he wouldn't like what he saw. He probably just feels sorry for me and is trying to make me feel better after having had such a bad day.

"Let's ask for a box and I will let you drop me off at my mother's house."

"That won't work."

"Why not?"

"I have 21 hours left to fulfill my commitment and I am a man of my word.

"No, really, you have been more than kind and I am fine."

"I agree."

"Great, then let's go."

"I agree with what you said. I have been more than kind and you are fine. Very fine." That grin spread across his face again.

"Be real! 21 hours will be noon tomorrow. You can't stay up all night. Don't you have a job or a life or something?"

"I'm free. I couldn't live with myself if something were to happen to you on my watch."

"I'm fine ... (Remembering the embarrassing exchange, she quickly tried to avoid the trigger word.) "Nothing bad is going to happen to me."

"I'll bet you didn't anticipate the bad events that happened to you thus far. I'll be here to protect you as long as you need me."

"I don't need you to protect me. I don't need anyone."

"Okay, I'll leave when my commitment is up."

"To be honest, this is a little creepy. Why such an interest in me?"

"The fact that you have to ask only makes you more interesting to me."

"Who are you? I don't even know your name."

"We have all night. Let's try and guess each other's name."

"Look, this day has been... well my brain feels like

scrambled eggs."

"Uh, oh, that means I need to extend my hours of observing you, Laven."

"Wait, how do you know my name?"

A grin played on his face. "Don't look at me like I am psychic or a ...stalker.

"Your purse."

"You looked in my purse? How dare you!"

"Not in your purse. I couldn't help noticing the little charm dangling there. It told me your name."

"Hold on, are you the one?"

"I certainly could be. What are my prospects?"

"Are you the one who crashed into me?"

"No, I was an innocent by-stander, an eye witness to the collision."

"Where is the car?"

"I had it towed to the shop. I am quite sure it's

totaled. I hope you don't mind."

"No, and I hope the rental company won't mind that I wrecked it either."

"You didn't wreck it. The other driver, a female slammed into you. It almost appeared that she did it intentionally and then left the scene. She was driving an all-terrain vehicle without a license plate. It's all in the police report."

"I would really like to go ho... I mean to her place. Could you please just drop me off? I have so many thoughts spinning around in my mind and I need to sort them out."

"I thought we had established that I am a man of my word. In order to keep my integrity, I need to fulfill my oath to watch you for a full 24 hours."

"Why don't we just exchange phone numbers? You can call me every hour on the hour to ensure that I am okay."

"The document I signed was not to converse via cell

phone on an hourly basis."

"I still don't know your name."

He hesitated. "It's J."

"Glad to meet you Jay. Do you have another name?

"I guess we are not on a last name basis. I don't have your last name."

"Hoddy"

"Laven Hoddy. It has a nice ring. Kind of like an exotic sports car.

"A sports car?"

"Something like Austin Healey, Lamborghini Aventador, Porsche Spyder, Ferrari Spider."

She giggled.

"Okay, those sound nothing like my name! I haven't even heard of most of them. Some sound like insects and others like repellent."

"Spiders are technically not insects but arachnids.

But that is funny!"

"Back to my name, there's an H in there that throws everything. Laven H. Hoddy."

"Hmmm, what is the H for?"

"Who knows? I guess my mother just tossed it in there as a bonus letter for me to decide what to do with it."

The silly talk and lighthearted conversation somehow made her feel more at ease. She had to control the urge to let her guard down. After all he remained a stranger.

"Jay what? Your other name?"

He studied her face for a moment, an extended moment. And then replied, "Shane."

"Jay Shane. What do you do for a living?"

"I don't live to work. "

Oh, so now I am getting the picture.   He is

unemployed. That explains the pathetic excuse for a
vehicle. He's a bum, a handsome bum, but a bum.

"You must be referring to my career."

"Exactly."

"I am in Real Estate."

"Oh, you are hoping to land a listing on my mother's
house. Well, I hate to disappoint you, but she could
have been renting for all I know. So if that's your
angle, you have wasted a lot of nice for nothing. I
will reimburse you for my dinner or can you use that
for a tax deduction?"

He laughed out loud. "Where did that come from?
Let me jog your memory. I didn't know about your
mother or her house until you told me a little while
ago. What do you mean my angle? Can't someone
do something nice for you without you suspecting
him of a selfish motive?"

"If that isn't it, then why are you going out of your
way for me?"

"Laven Hoddy, you have trust issues. You must have

been hurt deeply."

She said nothing but her lips didn't have to move, her eyes told him that hurt ran deeply into her soul.

He reached for her hand, but she withdrew it quickly like a wounded animal not wanting to be touched.

"Let me win your trust. I can be trusted and I will prove it."

His words pulled her emotions in different directions. She wanted to believe that someone would truly care about her, but why would he. She felt as though she would break in two from the pressure.

"Just please stop staring at me. Please take me to my mother's house."

"You have beautiful eyes. I can see goodness in them. They appear bottomless and draw me in while shutting me out at the same time. I see a deep hurt amongst the gold flecks."

"Well, the gold there is all the gold I possess, but I am loaded with problems. So please do us both a favor and ignore my issues and take me to Checquered Lane.

"Don't be so blinded by what was, that you can't recognize what is. You are broken but you don't have to stay that way. I don't know who injured you so badly, but not every body you meet has a hidden agenda.

You can trust me, Laven Hoddy." His eyes seemed to give her a virtual hug. "My new ride awaits us." He smiled and stood up from the booth and guided her out of the Sip and Chew Diner.

His words squeezed at her heart. If only she could believe they were real. If he is was real. If something sounds too good to be true…

Chapter 2

~~~

ABSENT OF STREET LAMPS, the dark blanket of night melted into the black asphalt leading to a structure that was once home to her mother. The large balding tree branches intertwined overhead to provide a tunnel-like canopy and prevented the moon's glow from peaking through.

"It's dark."

"Sure is. Time goes fast when you're enjoying the

company you're with."

The headlights wrestled to cut through the night and illuminate the road.

"The speed of light has been calculated."

"Yes it has. It travels at a speed of 187,000 miles per second. "

She glanced over and his smile seemed to be glowing in the dark.

"What are you, a Trivia Titan?"

"Hardly! I am a font of useless information." He grinned.

"You should go on a TV show, like Jeopardy or something?"

"I shy away from the limelight. I am more of a behind the scene kind of guy."

"What's the speed of dark?"

"Ha!"

"Are you certain this is even the street?"

Should I stay in a motel tonight? Would I be safer? I can't! This is my one and only opportunity to search for any hint of her rationale for abandoning me. There must have been a reason. I desperately need an explanation for why she withheld her love and refused mine. If ever answers can be found, it has to be now. It has to be here.

Laven's life had been motivated by distrust.

The nurse named Libby had assured her that this guy could be trusted, but no one assured her that I could trust the nurse's judgment.

She had always strategized a way out of facing hurt, a plan B. This may come in handy tonight.

She cautiously reached into her purse and pulled out a small black dual-purpose flashlight and placed it in her sweater pockets.

She did this not only for the light it could provide where there was none, but also for the secret Taser that could be switched on should she need one. Any malicious act toward her would be met with a zap that would send the one attempting it to the ground.

"You read the sign when we turned in."

"Yeah, the tiny one next to the large No Outlet sign."

I should feel uncomfortable. I am in a clunker car with a stranger traveling on a dark street in an unfamiliar town going who knows where.

I should feel uncomfortable, but surprisingly enough, I don't. Maybe because I am so beaten down from the day that my reliable defense mechanism is weakening. And maybe

it's my confidence in the flashlight, which performs a twofold purpose. Nevertheless, beware Laven.

"According to the GPS, we should be arriving momentarily."

She silently snickered that his phone was worth more than his car when she saw a light in a window. The house wouldn't have been visible without it.

"Look, I see a light. I was beginning to think nobody lived on this dreary street."

"Where?"

"Oh, it's gone. I'm sure I saw a light flicker right over there."

"It must have traveled 187,000 miles per second out of there because I'm not seeing it now. You saw it one second ago, right?

His humor made her feel like he doubted that she had seen a light. She was beginning to doubt it too.

"This is it. Prepare for landing."

The white two-story house stood out in the darkness.

Laven wondered why a woman alone would need a house this large. Had she lived here when Laven was squeezed into a bedroom with other foster kids as a teenager?

She came back to the present when Jay opened the

car door for her.

"I'll use the flashlight on my phone. Do you have a key?"

Her hand nervously fumbled in her purse for the key that her mother's nurse was instructed to give her.

"I hope there is electricity. It's so dark out here. It doesn't look like anyone else lives here."

"You saw a light."

"You mean the one that is 187,000 miles away from here." She said it with a tinge of sarcasm. He just showed his gorgeous teeth.

She was too nervous to fit the key into the lock. Her hands were shaking, but why? It wasn't like anyone was waiting to welcome her inside.

"Here, let me help," he offered as he opened the door. "And let there be light."

"Great! The electricity is on! At least one good thing has happened today."

"Is that the only good thing, Laven?"

How unappreciative that sounded.

Looking at the kindness in his eyes she wondered how she was going to tell him it was time for him to go. Did she really want him to go?

She was in this big house alone in the middle of nothing but dark.

Was she safer with him or without him?

"That didn't come out right. Of course, it's not the only good thing. You have been so thoughtful and I really appreciate it."

"I wouldn't have wanted to be anywhere else with anyone else."

"Let's look around before you have to go," she uttered with a silent groan.

"This place is big, but it won't take us that many hours to explore it.

The rooms were large and the fact that the furnishings were sparse gave it an empty, echoic feel.

"It doesn't look lived in."

"The 'less is more' theme is appealing to some."

"What is in here? With a flip of a switch, a kitchen appeared. Laven opened a cabinet door. "Corn Flakes."

"Did you know that there are more nutrients in the box than there is in the cereal?"

"I didn't know that. But nobody eats cornflakes without milk. Milk is full of vitamins and protein," she said as she continued to look in the cabinets.

"That's true, but why not just drink the milk and eat the carton. That way, no dirty bowl and spoon to wash."

Laven opened the refrigerator door. "It's cold but empty. There is no more food in here."

"Odd."

The dining room held a long table that hosted 10 chairs. Laven tried to picture her mother sitting there alone.

"There is nothing to personalize this place. I wonder if she really lived here?"

"Shall we go upstairs?"

Laven studied his face. That is where the bedrooms would be.

He saw her look and added, "To see what remains of the house."

"You go first and I will follow."

They had seen five bedrooms. Some had beds others did not.

Behind the final door, stood the most elaborately designed bed she had ever seen. It was antique most certainly and had to be one of a kind. The brass spiraled and spun around a circular frame that hosted a crystal glass plate in its center.

It was majestic and looked more like jewelry than a piece of furniture to sleep on. This was far too interesting for a good night's sleep. Beds should bore you to sleep. Following the twists and curls were sure to either hypnotize or gen up your imagination. The only salvation was that sleep usually happens in the dark with the lids of your eyes shut tight.

Four tall posts capped with balls coupled the head and the foot of the frame together.

Seven straight columns broke into the swirls on the footboard. The center one was composed of four smaller columns and stood with added importance in the line up.

"Beautiful!" Laven exclaimed.

"Looks like a museum piece."

"This must be the master bedroom."

It accommodated other massive wooden pieces.

Adjoining it was a bathroom with an oversized shower covered by an etched glass door on hinges, but no tub. Hadley was relieved to be escorted back down the stairs

"Have a seat," she said as she plopped down on the sofa. "Could I offer you some cornflakes since that is all we have. Oh, or better yet a bite of the box?"

He let out a laugh as he sat on the sofa near her. Laven stiffened. When she had offered him a seat, she was referring to the chair. She slid herself closer to the sofa's arm.

"I've noticed all the doors and windows have automatic locking features. Once closed they are locked."

"What does that mean?"

"It means that if you go outside and the door closes, you had better have a key or you aren't getting back in."

"I wonder why she had that type of locks installed?"

"Probably because it saved her from having to go around this large house and check to ensure that everything was locked. If they are closed, they are locked."

Laven wondered if there had been another reason. Perhaps she was afraid and felt this was extra security. Her mind drifted back to her mother.

"Are you okay?"

Laven nodded her head, "Yeah, why do you ask? For medical reasons?"

"You have sat there for awhile with a far away look in your eyes. You have had a very hard day. Do you want to talk about it?"

"No," but she spoke anyway, "My mother's last words keep playing over in my mind.

Her words were hard to understand, but it sounded like she said. 'Look at the mag…"

She stopped abruptly. Was this something she should share with him?

"What were her last words to you?"

Laven quickly looked away. "They were muffled and hard to understand. I do wish they would have held some value.

Maybe nothing she would have said to me would have been enough. I don't know how many words it would take to fill the hole that her years of silence has dug in me."

"Forgive her, Laven. Don't let your yesterdays eat

up all of your todays."

"Just like that. Wipe away years of neglect with one svelte swoop and 'poof ' it's gone? You just don't understand."

Shut up, Laven. You are opening up and sounding like the weak and rejected fool that you are and always will be.

"I want to understand you, Laven. Help me so I can help you."

For someone to want to help her, dug at her soul. But what if he wasn't genuine and was just spewing empty words? That would be more than she could endure. The risk was much too high a wager.

"Enough about me. Tell me about you."

Every time he grinned, it chipped at her internal armor.

 "Me?" I'm a very blessed guy- much more so than I deserve. I run pretty much counter to culture."

 "What do you mean?"

"Well, if the current culture says do it, I don't. And if it says don't, then I do. Everything is at odds with the way it was meant to be and I try to stand balanced as the world is tipping upside down trying to throw people in the wrong direction and off center."

"Hmm."

"All the labels are getting mixed up. Good is put on bad and bad is labeled good. I try to be a re-labeler."

She was beginning to wish she hadn't asked him to tell about himself. It felt like the more he spoke, the distance between them narrowed. She was pressed to the arm of the sofa on one side and him on the other. The only way of escape was up.

She stood.

She had to get him to leave. He had to go. She felt her defenses weakening and she was not about to set herself up for an epic fall. Life had already been too cruel. It would be pure stupidity to invite more pain.

She felt like if she allowed it, this could trump all her previous hurts.

"Do you mind terribly if we continue this at another time? I have a pile of thoughts to sort through and I would like to start off with a hot shower."

She stopped him before he could start. "I know you are a man of your word. Your kindness is more than I have ever experienced. I can't find the words that are able to demonstrate my gratitude…. I really need to be alone now."

He studied her face. "If you insist, Laven. Leave the door open for me."

"But"

He talked as he started for the door. "I will bring in your luggage. I pulled them from the wreckage before I had the car towed away."

Another act of thoughtfulness or had he had planned her rescue out thoroughly for reasons unknown?

She thanked him as he sat them inside the door.

"I will go, if you insist, but let me add my number to your favorites in your phone."

"I'll add it." She said as she pulled it from her sweater pocket.

"No," he gently lifted the phone from her hand. "Let me do it."

His thumbs navigated quickly through her phone. "No favorites?" "No entries?"

"No need. I told you before, I don't need anyone."

Laven noticed sadness in his eyes.

Oh, no you don't. You will not feel sorry for me.

"But, Laven, friends are a blessing."

"A blessing I don't need."

"Friends are put in your life for you to love and for them to love you back. You can't exist as an island."

"Maybe you can't, but don't speak for me. I have become quite adept at it."

His eyes were kind as he spoke. "You are injured and have been living a broken existence.

"Only when you are able to admit that you are broken can you begin to be fixed."

His words stung at her heart. They rang with truth.

"What are you trying to do, fix me like you are fixing your car? I am not your broken specimen to work on. Since you have me all figured out, please just go."

"I will be here for you if you need me. Trust me, Laven."

He handed her phone back to her with one contact number saved. She resisted the urge to delete it. The door closed behind him and locked.

I have saved myself the torture of increasing the pain in my heart. If someone seems too good to be true..

Chapter 3

~~~

SHE SAT ON THE sofa with her arms wrapped around her legs as tightly as possible, as if to hold herself in one piece. She felt like she was coming apart. All the day's happenings were whirling in her head.

"What does all this mean? My mother leaving and, with her, taking all possibilities of finally being part my life, being spared physical harm from a car wreck, and now this new man that she desperately wanted to believe and trust."

A lifetime of emotions had capsuled into one day.

A sudden loud bang and shattering of glass preceded a large rock crashing through the window and narrowly missing her.

Shocked, she stood over the rock. Written on it were the words, 'LEAVE to LIVE.'

She quickly called 911. Afraid to go near the broken window, she quickly carried the painted rock into the kitchen. As she studied the written warning, the letters began to fade and soon were completely vanished from sight. With shaky hands, she sat the rock on the floor and waited in the dark kitchen for the police.

It seemed an eternity before a knock finally sounded. Flashing red and blue lights gave Laven the signal that it was safe to come out of the dark and approach the front door. Trembling, she showed the policemen the window and led them to the projectile that sat innocently on the floor.

The police officer picked up the rock with protected hands.

"You told dispatch that there was a warning with it. Where is the warning?"

Just as she was about to answer, a knock pounded on the door. The other policeman left to see who was there. He returned with another person and they entered the kitchen.

Laven stared at Jay. She was glad to see him. "There were words written on the white painted patch, but now they are gone. There were words written in blue. They said, 'Leave to Live'. It was a threat!" Laven spoke somewhat breathlessly.

"The policemen exchanged glances. "The letters were there and now they are gone?"

"That's right." Thinking they doubted her story, she quickly looked toward Jay.

"She has had a very difficult day. She was struck by a hit and run driver and now this." Jay entered the conversation.

"Who are you?" The first policeman questioned. The second policeman smiled and nodded as if he already knew him.

"I am a friend." Jay shot a glance toward Laven. "I brought her home from the hospital earlier tonight."

The first policeman handed the heavy stone to his counterpart who also wore gloves and jotted something on a form.

"What do you think? I made this whole thing up? Do you think I threw the rock through the window myself? Do you think I wrote the threat on it and then cleaned it off before you got here?"

"We are just going through the formalities ma'am."
The rock is too heavy for you to have thrown
through the upper portion of the window. We will
take the stone back to headquarters for
examination and have it checked for fingerprints. In
the meantime, we will patrol the area. Are you
going to be okay?"

"Well, it just depends on if the threat is serious and
how long the one who wrote the threat gives me to
leave." Laven was frustrated and felt that she wasn't
believed.

"Could you please sign here? " Laven skimmed over
the form and reluctantly signed her name and stood
silently as she watched them pull their patrol car
away.

"Do you believe me, Jay?"

"I have no reason not to." He reached to give her a
hug but she quickly pulled away.

*Wait a minute. The rock was too heavy for me to
throw, but He could have thrown it. He hadn't
wanted to leave. Maybe this was his ticket back into
the house.*

"You sure got here quickly. How did you know

something was wrong?"

"I had just gotten around the corner at the end of the road when I saw the patrol cars turn in with their lights on so I turned around and came back to make sure you were okay."

"I'm not delusional, Jay. One moment the words were there as plain as day and the next they were gone. It happened fast."

"The speed of light fast?"

Was he referencing the light I saw earlier? Does he think I am seeing things that aren't really there? Does he think I am crazy? Am I crazy? Did the knock on my head make me see things? Was this one of the symptoms the Doctor warned about?

"Just long enough for me to read them. By the time I hung up the phone they were gone. Either some juvenile delinquent is playing pranks or it was a threat."

"It is too late to get the window fixed so I am going to stay here tonight. You go up and get your shower and some rest. I will stand guard down here. Well, maybe sit guard." He teased. "There is a lock on the master bedroom door."

Was he staying because he believes I am in danger or is he staying because he thinks my brain is behaving in a dysfunctional manner? Either way, I am not going to argue.

"Thank you! Tomorrow you can have your life back."

"Tomorrow, we will get the window fixed and get you some groceries. Those cornflakes won't last long even with the box. Good night. Call if you need me."

"Good night." She said as she picked up the smaller suitcase and started upstairs. He made a motion to help her, but she stopped him. "I am fi... I can make it.

Do you need a blanket?"

"I have a jacket in the car. Get some rest. You have more than earned it."

~

The shower would have to take a rain check. Laven's emotional roller coaster ride came to an abrupt stop on top of an overstuffed feather pillow.

The hands on the clock had ticked off a full circle. She couldn't believe that her deep sleep had lasted 12 hours. The sun peeked through the slits of the wooden plantation shutters. She was rested and ready to face a new day with whatever surprises awaited her. The old one hadn't destroyed her and what doesn't do you in, serves to strengthen you.

She turned the shower to hot and selected the strongest water flow available. She was ready to bring the day on and stare it down. She wasn't crazy and she was going to succeed in proving it.

While drying, she heard her name drift up from downstairs.

She threw on her beige chenille robe, white furry slippers, wrapped the large white towel around her head, and walked down the stairs to see why Jay was calling her.

There were four remaining stairs before the living room floor met her furry feet. She stopped in disbelief. There was no longer broken glass on the floor. There was no longer a broken window.

"It's fixed!"

"If you are referring to my new car, not yet."

"The window! Thank you! I'm sorry I slept so long. How much do I owe you?"

Jay's face broke into an irresistible smile.

Why is he smiling so big? She looked down to make certain there were no gaps or openings in her robe and she was covered where she should be.

"What?" She quizzed.

"You look like a vanilla ice cream cone."

She stood still in her beige robe and felt of the swirled white towel on her head and almost felt like an ice cream cone. His warm smile was about to melt her. She quickly turned to go back up the stairs, but one of her slippers slipped off

"Maybe that's why they call them slippers," she said as she fumbled to return her foot inside it.

"That is a genuine Cinderella move if I have ever seen one! Same shoes, same moves." He grinned.

"Only I am not silly enough to wear glass slippers."

"Neither was Cinderella. In the original story, her slippers were white fur probably provided by a couple of unlucky squirrels."

"Are you kidding? You have already ruined cornflakes for me. Please don't start on my fairly tales."

"Sorry, it was a mistranslation. The French words *'pantoufles en vair'* (slippers made of white squirrel fur) and *'pantoufles en verre'* (slippers made of glass) got mixed up and her wardrobe accessories changed for countless generations.

For the squirrels' sake, I prefer the glass version. I am trusting that yours are faux.'

She nodded and started once again to climb the stairs.

"Wait! It's your phone. I heard you stirring around up there and wanted you to know that you had a phone call." He handed the phone up to her and she hurried back to the master bedroom.

She waited until she was dressed to return the call.

"Hello, I missed a call from this number."

"Is this Laven Hoddy?"

"Yes, it is."

"Hello, Miss Hoddy, I am your mother's attorney and executor of her will. I am from out of town and would like to meet with you today and read to you your mother's last will and testament."

"What time would you like to meet?"

"At 1:30 p.m., if possible. It would allow me time for an early evening flight back."

"I believe that will work. At least I think I have a ride. If not, I will call you back in 10 minutes. What is the address?"

"I will text you the address. Please understand this is temporary, as my office isn't in this state and I haven't any local associates. We need more privacy than a restaurant would afford."

"I'll see you at 1:30."

"That will be fine. Good day!"

Laven caught herself taking extra time in front of the mirror. Was it to look professional in the presence of the attorney or was it to garner extra attention from her new...friend? The thought made her angry at herself. No! She refused to go down a one-way street to heart break. It doesn't matter what I look like. Beauty is only skin deep and it wouldn't take long to discover that what her skin was covering was not pretty. She messed up her hair in defiance.

She flung her purse over her shoulder, grabbed her sweater and headed for the staircase. On the way down, the ring tone sounded indicating the arrival of a text message. She stopped at the bottom of the stairs to read it.

"It's my mother's attorney. He wants to meet me at 1:30 to read her will."

"What's his name? I might know him."

She scrolled down the message and read his name aloud.

"Ha, Ha!! You are joking, right?"

"No, why? Do you know him?"

"Come on! Larceny Crook? Ha, Ha!"

She smiled and began to laugh along.

He continued to laugh. "Did he ask if your refrigerator was running?"

"Calm down." It was difficult to read through her

giggles. "Listen!" She spelled out,

"L, A, R, S, O, N,   E.   C,R,U.Q,U,E. "It's French I think. Maybe I am pronouncing it incorrectly."

"If anyone is a candidate for a name change, he would rank up there," he said, beginning to wind down his laughter.

"There is a Dr. Payne where I live. Would it be too much to ask for a ride to meet with him?"

"You want to meet with Dr. Payne?"

No, No, Mr. Cruque."

"It would be my pleasure. And then we will pick up some groceries. In fact, we have time to stop for some… " He stopped to look at his watch, "Brunch on the way."

"Thank you!"

"Don't forget the key. Remember the doors are trained to lock themselves."

She was overly conscience of his fingers on her elbow as he guided her down the porch steps. A warmth radiated through her. She quickly pulled away as they walked to his oxidized, beat up car.

"Hey, you fixed my seat belt!"

"As you lay sleeping."

"You fixed it in the dark?"

"No, early this morning. I took the latch from the back seat and bolted it up here. All so you could ride safely."

Looking around at the missing knobs and red warning lights on the instrument panel, she decided it might take more than tightening down a bolt to make this beater, better.

"We are in the country." She announced as she observed Cherquered Lane with the benefit of the daylight.

"Although it is rural, it is still within Rising Falls city limits."

Laven looked in the area where she had spotted the light the night before. Though the house sat a ways off of the road, she thought she saw a movement of a curtain, maybe a breeze.

BAM! A gunshot! The loud explosion stole her breath.

"Where did that come from?!"

"You are shaking," he said, as he rested his hand over hers.

"Someone is shooting at us!" she stammered.

"No, no, the car backfired. I need to check the ignition wiring. Or the catalytic converter could be damaged, if it is even there."

As he spoke, she slowly pulled her hand from beneath his.

Still shaken, she said. "If you didn't have to haul me around, you'd have the time to work on the fix-it list for your new car."

Remembering last night, she wondered if he was working on her. The thought irritated her.

I am nobody's project! Besides, some things are broken beyond repair. All I can do is guard against further damage. I can't, I won't let down my defenses.

When I return home, I'll send him a nice thank you note with a check to cover the fuel and other expenses along with some extra for his kindness.

God knows he can use the money. He obviously isn't at all successful in the real estate industry. If he uses this vehicle to show properties to prospective buyers, it's no surprise.

"A penny for your thoughts."

"You can't afford to get into my head," she played, still considering how unsuccessful he was.

"Inflation."

"I'm enjoying the scenery. This is a pretty town, very quaint. These lovely antique houses remind me of dollhouses. All the lawns are manicured. It shows pride of ownership."

"There is a lot of history here in Rising Falls. I would like to give you a tour.

We could visit the falls that appear to be going upward. The visual phenomenon has become quite a tourist attraction. People who travel to see the Changing of the Leaves festival in our neighboring city, Lake Haven, on the other side of the bridge, make it a priority to visit the falls also."

"That would be nice, if I have time before I have to leave."

"When are you leaving?"

"As soon as possible. I will have a clearer picture of my time frame after I hear the will." Her thoughts were interrupted.

A car pulled up in the adjacent lane. The driver was beating on the horn like it was a drum. They lowered the window and motioned for him to do the same. There were children in the backseat waving and displaying big smiles.

"I think they are trying to get your attention." She stated the obvious. He made no movement so she continued, "It looks like they want to tell you something."

She felt sorry for him. It was no doubt that the commotion was about this horrible excuse of an automobile, but he wasn't going to take the bait. The kids were laughing and making driving antics.

"They are just trying to be friendly. It's refreshing to find nice people."

He pressed on the accelerator and the car responded with yet another loud explosion-like sound. He grinned and hurried away without learning what all the attention-grabbing motions were about. She looked over her shoulder at the woman in the passenger seat. There she sat, as if upon a throne, in her beautiful shiny car, making fun of someone less fortunate by displaying an obnoxious thumb up motion. Laven found it to be neither nice nor friendly. She found it to be mean-spirited.

"I wonder what that was all about? Are you going to pull over to see if something is wrong?" When the words were spoken, she remembered it would be more noteworthy to find something right about this car.

"You know, there is an epidemic of rudeness that is spreading and infecting the people across this country. To be insulting is applauded as quick-witted. Low, surly sarcasm is touted as a skill. Crude, raw, obscene language is being widely accepted even when it comes from the lips of the fairer gender. It is expected to be treated discourteously and impolitely. Don't say anything politically incorrect, but to be inconsiderate of others is overlooked."

It wasn't the response she had expected. "I'll take that as a 'no'." she said carefully.

"Take it as a 'YES', a prompting for us to be positive. 'Yes' is more powerful and contagious than the 'no' of rudeness. We can turn it around."

Laven was swimming in the pool of his numerous words. The one that floated to the top was 'we'. What did that mean? It excited parts of her, but other parts were fighting against the word.

There is no plural for me, no 'we'. To think that I could be a 'we' with this person is tragically laughable. Was it, then, the car? Was he attempting with all of his words to change the subject?

She was wondering if he was truly insulted by the people in the shiny new vehicle and in reality didn't find them kind nor friendly but rude. It would be delusional to think otherwise.

A smile spread across his face. It was the first time she had seen it from a side view.

Still good.

"One of the highest highs you can catch comes from doing something for someone who you know will never be able to pay you back." Like a ventriloquist, he spoke the words without interrupting the unbelievable smile.

If he thinks this is one of his highs, he is mistaken. I can and will repay him for all he has done for me.

"Lunch or brunch is on me," she announced when the car rattled into the parking space of the restaurant. There was a vacancy rumble coming from her tummy, but by the looks of this place, an appetizer might have to suffice. His vehicle stood out, not like a sore, but like a mutilated thumb against all the expensive cars in the lot. Of course this car might even look bad in a salvage yard.

Chapter 4

~~~

LAVEN WAS IN AWE when she stepped inside the elegant restaurant. In front of her stood a spectacular glass wishing well. The glass was crystal clear with bubbling water swishing through the walls. The effervescing bubbles sparkled with the constant changing of rainbow colors. A hologram rested magically over the glass roof of the well, projecting the name of the restaurant, 'Well Wishes'. She peeked over the high edge and saw piles of coins. She had the urge to throw in a handful, but a second thought reminded her that she might need every penny to pay for their meal.

Still mesmerized, she didn't move until Jay pulled her toward the waiter who then escorted them to their table.

After being seated in the posh, private booth, Jay held up his hand in a friendly manner to let the waiter know that there would be no need for menus.

"The usual?" The waiter returned his smile.

"Yes, actually two. One for the lady, also."

The usual?! If he frequented this expensive restaurant, there was no mystery as to why he had to drive that piece of rubbish car.

"I hope you don't mind me ordering for you. I believe you will like it. If not, we will get you something different."

Don't mind? I didn't even get a look at the menu to see the price!

"It's fine, but fast food would have been satisfactory for me." She wondered if the growl in her stomach was from internal dollar signs stomping around.

"You deserve a nice meal."

"Like I deserved a twelve hour rest?   This is a very nice place. It has such a wonderful ambiance. The name really fits it. "

She looked around at the framed calligraphy letters spelling out phrases of encouragement.

Her eyes followed the polished wooden arches that reached to the high ceiling, which was exquisitely painted to appear as a golden sky at twilight. Over each booth dangled a crystal pendant lamp leaning toward the art deco style.   In the center of the restaurant   dangled   a   massive,   ornate   iron chandelier   arrayed   in   rectangular   crystals demanding attention. If competing with the wishing well though, it might just as well be a camping lantern, she thought.

"I love the wishing well! I want to throw money in there just to compensate for entertaining me with its beauty!"

He smiled, "In that case, you also deserve a tip."

Laven lowered her eyes.

He is staring at me again.

"You can feed it some coins on the way out. All the money people put in there goes to the Boy's Ranch to help homeless and under privileged boys."

At the speed of light, Laven's thoughts took her back to the orphanage where she had grown up. They had the bare necessities.

Sundays were special because that was the day that they were served real meat. Soups and casseroles containing no meat or mystery meat of some kind was served on the other days. All girls lived in her building. The boys lived in the adjoining building.

"Why the sad face? I thought you liked the wishing well."

Laven quickly corrected the look on her face. "Oh, I do, it's just that..."

"Don't worry, Laven. I am going to pick up the bill for this." He grinned.

"And just what makes you think you are more able to afford this meal than I am?"

She was both relieved and insulted.

"Because I get a huge discount here and you don't."

"Why, do you have a coupon or something?"

"I work here."

"You are kidding, right?"

"No, I really do."

"What's your job here?"

"Mostly dishwasher and some janitorial."

His vehicle of transportation was making more sense now. "But I thought you worked in real estate." She looked at him warily.

"I just work here when they are short- handed. I am not so good as a waiter and forget the prep cook position, but I am pretty good at washing dishes."

Before Laven could comment, their meal was presented to them.

"Can I get you a drink?" The waiter addressed Laven.

"No, thank you, I don't drink."

Jay threw her a smile. "You drink water. I've seen you." Please let the pretty lady experience some mint tea. Shall we pray."

Laven felt more than uncomfortable praying in public and with the waiter standing there. She bowed her head anyway as Jay asked for a blessing over the server whose name was John and he prayed that things would go well for her at the meeting with the attorney.

When he finished, she glanced around to see if they had caused a scene, but no one seemed to notice. All was well.

"This is beautiful! It looks like a piece of art. I hate to mess it up." She said as she scooped up her first bite. She waved at him with her eyes closed and her mouth full. "Scrumptious!" She continued to remark with each mouthwatering bite. "Hmmm,

Splendid!! Amazing!"

"Now describe the food."

Oh, no not this again. I refuse to let him ruin this delicious meal with embarrassing comments. There

is time to be embarrassed later. I might never have food this good again!

"This is the yummiest food I have ever had. It's well seasoned and savory. It's beyond delicious! Plus, everything is always better when you get it at a bargain."

"Funny, you should say that. This whole place was a bargain.

It was built on a prayer and a vision. The building sat empty for years so the city sold it for the taxes levied against it. The décor was bought at auction, scavenged before a casino was imploded. It cost a small fraction of what a franchise for a fast food restaurant would have been. "

"Hearing that is like seeing how the special effects of a movie was achieved.

It walks away with the fun," she offered while enjoying each and every bite of food.

"I thought you liked a bargain."

"I do, but this is the nicest restaurant that I have

ever been in. I don't want the experience to be shrunk."

"Ha. Well, if it keeps your experience from shrinking, the wishing well is an original, specially constructed, and, not by any measure, cheap."

Laven smiled as she finished the last mouthful of food from her plate.

"In case, you didn't know, that was delicious!!"

John returned with the check and a small silver platter holding two candies that were covered in what looked like red Christmas wrapping paper. Before she had a chance to look at the bill's total, Jay offered his credit card and the waiter walked away.

"They are double wrapped. Open it," he said handing her one of the candies.

Laven slowly pulled the red foil wrapper off and a note fell out.

She unfolded it and read, "**A Life Without God is a Lonely Life. He Loves You. He is Waiting. Reach for**

Him Today." She folded the small strip of paper and put it in her purse.

"What did yours say?" Jay asked, already munching on his chocolate candy.

"That is a can I don't want to open today." She answered wondering if he had something to do with the message she received.

"You can read mine." Handing it to her added, "Why don't you go out by the wishing well while I wait to pay."

"Thanks, I will, after a quick stop in the lady's room." She glanced around at the other tables and the ones finished had all received the red covered chocolates. It must be the Well Wishes' version of a fortune cookie.

The beautiful glass wishing well was no less fascinating than its first viewing. She pulled out her change purse and emptied the contents into the deep well and watched as the dancing bubbles changed colors.

Touching the glass confused her senses; bubbles

should be wet even if they were a shade of violet turning magenta.

She thought of the little boys this change would benefit and hoped they would find a happy life. Her heart went out to them.   There was an atmosphere here in this place that made her not want to leave.

"Shall we go?"

She looked at him with a 'do we have to' look.

"We have just enough time to make it the attorney."

The car backfired as they pulled out of the parking lot. This time Laven wasn't startled.

She wondered how long before it made one last explosion and refused to move again. Would it even be worth anything for parts?

She smiled at Jay.

"Doesn't scare you anymore?"

"Guess not."   She glanced at the quaint little main street lined with matching green and white striped canopies and thought about the rock with the warning.

That did scare her. She hoped she could get some closure from this meeting and be on her way out of this strange, little town with the crazy name.

"Are you sure you have the correct address?"

Laven checked the text message. "Yes, this is it. "

It was a dark building on the outskirts of town and suite 7 turned out to be a small motel room."

"I am so glad you came with me."

"That's what friends are for." He smiled.

She knew it was a jeer for her proclamation of not needing friends.

"I am a friend you know. If you don't believe me just look in your phone contact list."

He doesn't know that I almost deleted it.   The thought gave her a one up on him but she wouldn't tell him.

"Are you nervous?"

"Yes, a little."

"I will stand outside the door to give you privacy, but I'll be close if you need me." He told her as he walked her to room 7.

She stepped inside the dimly lit room. The bed had been pushed up against the wall and a small desk placed in front of it. A chair had been positioned on the other side of the desk for her to sit in.

A nameplate was sitting on the desk as if to make the shabby room look professional. It read Larson Ernest Cruque, confirming she was in the right place. Just then the bathroom door opened and a man stepped out and entered the make shift office.

She gasped when her eyes encountered the man.

He was remarkable, wearing what appeared to be a fantastic off the shelf costume. If his name was a play on words then his appearance was a play on sight. His countenance contradicted reality. Was he for real or trying to play a practical joke on her? She was uncertain as to whether she should be amused or pity the man.

Gray thickets of bushy eyebrows obstructed his sight, so much so that he had to tilt his head back in order to look someone in the eye. She fought the urge to suggest that gardening the hedges would avoid the wear on his long neck.

It was as though an ace bandage was stretched tightly over his bones.

His body was so devoid of substance that a ravenous carnivore wouldn't think him worth the effort and would pass him by. He nervously pulled at his king-sized mustache that covered his mouth in the same way his eyebrows covered his eyes.

She wondered if the explosion of facial hair was sucking out all nutrients keeping him in his emaciated looking state.

 When he threw his head back to look at her, Laven cast her eyes away trying to hide the fact that she had been staring.

"Miss Hoddy?"

"Yes.

"Have a seat please."

"Just a minute." She turned without having to take a step and opened the door. She grabbed Jay by his arm and pulled him into the room.

"And who is this?" inquired the man behind the desk.

"He's my…. " The words caught in her throat.

Jay gave her a continue motion with his hand. *He is going to make me say it!*

 "He's my friend. I would like him to be with me when the will is read."

"Very well. There is only one chair, but I can sit on the edge of the bed and he can have this chair."

Seeing him struggle at it clumsily, Jay lifted the chair easily over the desk. "Thank you."

"It will take me a moment here to get things in order."

Of all the estate attorneys, Larson E.

Cruque was her mother's choice to be the executor of her will! He was about to announce her mother's wishes for what she wanted done with the things she left behind, the things that no longer mattered.

Could Laven dare to hope that there would be something said that mattered to her?

Tugging at his bush of a mustache with one hand, he twirled his pen like a baton with the other. "At the time of her death, your mother's estate consisted of a house on 6336 Chequered Lane. "

He tilted his head back so that he could make eye contact and, like the conductor of an orchestra, he pointed the baton of a pen at Laven and then, with a jerk, pointed it across the room.

He then peered in that direction as if someone were actually seated there.

The house at said address will be donated to an unnamed benefactor who will in turn use it for the housing and training of rescued girls. It will be named, Daughters of Destiny, from Ashes to Gold.

Laven spoke out. "Oh, that is one rich irony!

She threw away her own daughter, and then had the love and compassion to help other people's daughters."

She looked at Jay and he had a started look on his face. Was he surprised at her outburst or was he disappointed in not being able to sell the house?

Mr. Cruque spoke, "Mothers are either vilified or sanctified. There is more."

He pointed the baton toward Laven. "To you, she left her antique brass bed. You are not to sell it, but take it with you. She left money to have it shipped."

Laven looked down, not wanting to have another emotional outpouring. "Are we finished here?"

"She also left you her poodle."

"What!!"

"Yes. Here is the check for the shipping of the bed and instruction concerning her ashes. My condolences on your loss."

I would rather have condolences on my gain. A bed I don't need and a dog I don't want.

Chapter 5

~~~

IT WAS SLENCE IN the car.

"I'm guessing you don't feel like grocery shopping."

"Hollow."

Jay looked at her puzzled.

"The extra H in my name, it is for Hollow. I am empty."

He tried to touch her hand, but she folded her arms.

I feel like there is a cylinder running through my core that has an antimagnetic force field that resists anyone coming near me. The cylinder is void of any contents. I am empty.

Laven's head was churning as they turned down Chequered Lane.

She did own the house. She didn't want me in her

house then. She doesn't want me in her house now. The estate gave me until the end of the month to leave. I'll be out of here at the end of the day tomorrow.

She shrugged off the movement she saw in the house that sat off the road.

Jay interrupted the silence. "I wonder what they are doing here?"

"The police! Maybe they found who threw the rock."

Laven was pleased to see them walking around the yard when the schlocky car clunked up to the house. "Any luck on finding the source of the threat?"

"We will provide information as we get it, but for today, we need to get your finger prints."

"To distinguish mine from the perpetrator? I regret touching the rock."

"Miss Hoddy, do you realize you were driving a stolen car?"

"A stolen car? No! It was a rental car! The rental agreement was in the glove box."

"The papers are for 'On Your Way', a company that does not exist."

"The man wasn't at a kiosk. I thought he was just being a proactive sales person, making it more convenient by coming to the customer."

"Can you give us a description?"

"Tall, medium build, very dark eyes. It almost looked like he was wearing eyeliner."

"Would you prefer to give your prints out here or go inside?"

"Are you arresting me?"

"No, but we will most likely have additional questions for you."

Great! The threatener said leave. The cops say don't.

"We will need a picture ID. Your drivers license will do."

She looked at Jay, "Do I need an attorney?"

"You have nothing to hide, Laven. They can

compare your prints to any on the rock or car."

The policeman said, " You aren't being accused, but we just need to get a few answers."

Laven unlocked the door. The officers and Jay followed her inside. The door locked behind them.

Her fingers were pressed straight down and then rolled. She was in a daze as they wiped the ink off of each finger with an alcohol pad when finished.

The dream of finally getting to meet her mother had warped into a nightmare! She had gone from a girl who minded her own, boring business to a suspected auto thief.

Jay was the only good thing that had happened to her but, for all she knew, he could be part of this strange twist of events. One more complication to endure and she would be free of all of this and could forget it had ever happened. She could try to forget that she had never had a mother.

The police officers thanked her and assured her that they would be in contact. She sat on the sofa and stared at nothing. She could vaguely overhear Jay reminding the uniformed visitors that an unlicensed vehicle had hit her, but she did notice him handing them a folded piece of paper.

"Have you questioned the neighbors?" She spoke as they walked out the door.

Jay walked over and sat down on the sofa. She would have preferred that he had sat on the chair.

"I'm sorry you are having such a rough time. After sitting silently beside her for an unmeasured amount of time, he continued. "Is there anything I can do for you?"

Laven's answer was weak and exhausted. "Thanks for the wonderful lunch and being with me at the freaky reading of the will, but I just need to be alone now."

"Are you sure that is what you really need?"

"Yes."

"Did you know that being totally alone increases mortality by 26 per cent?"

"Then I will look for something that works faster. I am hoping the end of all of this is better than the start. Please, Jay, go."

"Talking like that is no way to get me to go. You can't desire an ending when you've never found the beginning. You have been so eaten up by the past that you haven't found life. You are cutting donuts in a wasteland of what was."

"I'll be okay. I just need to be alone right now. My mother dealt me a gut punch from beyond, someone is throwing large stones at me, and the cops think I am a car thief. All my life I have made it my objective to stay below the radar. If you are quiet and mind your own business then you aren't targeted. Coming to this place has made me become a target. And to worsen the matter, on one hand, I am told I shouldn't leave and on the other I am told that I must leave if I want to live .

I have a target on my back and another on my front. There seems to be serious ramifications either way."

"If you let me stay, I promise to keep my mouth shut and stay out of your way."

Laven shook her head. "No, I need to be alone and try to straighten this curled up mess out. If I had my supplies, I might try to paint. That sometimes helps me release anxiety."

"You are an artist?"

"No, I just paint, in oil, but I am not very good at it."

"What do you like to paint? Still life?"

"Oddly enough, portraits. I try to avoid people, but I find facial features very interesting and I like to paint them. I enjoy dabbling in color and controlling the brush."

"I enjoy being a paintbrush in the hand of God and giving Him control. Like art, life is a blank canvas, raw material. It's in our hands to work it into beauty or ugliness."

"An artist is only as good as the material he has to work with. Some in life come better equipped than others."

"That's true to a point. But the one who can make a work of art out of rubble is the true artist."

"To whom much is given, much is required. Luke 12:48." The phrase came out of her mouth like a recording.

"I am impressed! Did you know that Peter Parker borrowed that scripture in Spiderman when he said, 'With great power comes great responsibility?'"

Before she could respond, he continued. "Remember though, God promised to supply our supplies. Philippians 4:9 says He will give us all our needs according to his riches in glory."

I wonder why he doesn't call down some of that for a much-needed car.

"You know scripture!"

"More than I ever really wanted to know."

"What do you mean?"

"My foster father exercised his considerable power and espoused that the partaking of the spiritual bread of life was more important than the temporal physical bread."

"You make him sound like a dictator. Was he strict?"

"'Eat the bread of life first', he would say.

He motivated us to learn the Bible by denying us dinner until we could quote, word for word, from the King James Version, his selected passages."

"What a negative approach. Wonder if he ever read Matthew 18:6 where it tells that anyone who hurts one of God's little ones better to wish for a millstone around his neck and to be thrown into the sea, because that would be a blessing compared to what God has waiting for him?"

"I think it was a power thing for him. They were obviously opening their house to foster kids only for financial gain. "

"Laven, I'm sorry that your introduction to God's word was so contrary to what God intended. I don't know your foster father's intentions, but what he did was to take life-giving words that bring blessing and hope and make them an instrument of dread.

"Yeah, I guess you could say I am fed up with scripture."

"Laven, do you know God?"

"Are you in the room? I just told you that I had the Bible forced down me in my formative years! I had no choice unless I chose not to eat. I know all about God."

"I didn't ask if you knew about Him. I asked if you knew Him. There is a universe of difference. Do you know who the first President of the United States was?"

She smirked. "Of course, George Washington."

"He was actually the 9th President of the United States. John Hansen was the first. George was the first president after the constitution was ratified."

"More useless info from your font?"

Jay smiled widely but his face soon became serious. Unlike George, God isn't a historical figure. He is here with us now. You can't just read about Him to know Him. No one can really know God until they have been touched by Him, until they have a personal relationship with Him. Most of us don't reach for or really get to know Him until we are at a breaking point."

"Look, Jay, I am in no mood for a history lesson nor a sermon for that matter. I'll walk you to the door."

"Laven, when you get to the end of yourself, God will be there waiting for you. He can turn all the bad things that have happened to you around for your good."

He paused at the door. "God will turn that H for Hollow into H for Hope."

His soft smile seared into her brain as the door locked behind him.

She gathered her purse and sweater and climbed the stairs. Once inside the master bedroom, she locked the door. All the doors and windows were locked tight, but she needed more protection. She had to tighten the lock on her heart.

Her defenses were easing and she couldn't let that happen. Believing hope was possible was an invitation for a destroying hurt.

She plopped herself down on her brass inheritance and decided that H was for Hurt. It was already there, but she wouldn't let it destroy her by believing hope was real. As painful as it was, she would lock herself even tighter and remained in hurt's familiar grip.

She opened her purse and pulled out the forgotten piece of candy from the Well Wishes restaurant. She popped it into her mouth and the rich milk chocolate's delicious taste felt as smooth as silk on her tongue. She pulled out the strip of paper that had rested beside the candy, unfolded it and once again read its message.

"A Life Without God is a Lonely Life. He Loves You. He is Waiting. Reach for Him Today."

Had to be staged!

She crumpled the strip of paper and threw it on the floor as she rose from the bed. In the nightstand drawer, she found a tablet and pen. With them in hand she started out of the room. Unlocking the bedroom door reminded her that she should have her purse with her at all times; without the house key, there was no returning inside should she decide to step out. The bedroom door stood open and unlocked but her heart was locked tighter than ever.

100

Chapter 6

~~~

LAVEN STUDIED HER REFLECTION in the mirror. She tossed a section of her long strawberry blonde hair out of the way. It was that long silver streak that she always played with when she was thinking or when she was nervous. Some days more red showed through, but other days the blonde won out. Maybe it was just her, but on occasions, mousy brown undertones seemed to overpower the lighter shades. Perhaps, like a mood ring, her hair changed with her temperament. Just like herself, nothing was definite about her hair.

She always admired dark hair, but was thankful it

didn't grow out of her own head. She felt her shade more easily blended in and commanded less attention no matter the mood. The only thing about her hair that stood out was that silly silver streak.

Trying to determine what combination of colors would be needed to create their likeness on canvas, she stared at the reflection of her own eyes. It would take white mixed with a dab of green and a hint of blue to accomplish the pale teal background and then small bits of yellow and tawny ochre to recreate the gold specks.

Her lashes were long and much darker than her hair but kept quiet without mascara. She glanced at her naturally arched brows and followed down her nicely shaped nose to her full lips.

Enough of looking at nothing!

After searching every space covered by a door or drawer for anything that might speak for her mother, she crawled on the floor and shined her dual-purpose flashlight under every bed. There was nothing behind any stick of furniture save a few dust bunnies. She found nothing so far with a tiny keyhole that might welcome her miniature key. At the end, she looked at her empty hands and felt a pain in her empty heart.

Is there nothing you left me here? Why did I…

A loud squeaking sound interrupted her thought.

She stepped on and off the guilty board in the floor like she was attempting a tune. She dropped to her knees and began to pry at the board until one corner lifted. Finally, the entire plank lifted revealing what had been hidden beneath it. Laven pulled out a book that had been propped on its edge out of the hole. Excitement lifted her to her feet when she found it was a scrapbook. Her mother must have procured pictures from the nuns and compiled a memory book for her.

If she had built mountain high expectations before, it was no comparison to the gaping crevice in which her disappointment plunged her. If visible, it would make the Grand Canyon look like a wrinkle.

This book was not made for her; it was not about her. It was about some girl by the name of Jessica, a red haired girl who someone actually cared about.

In saddened defeat, she walked, beaten, to the

bedroom for an empty pad and pencil and headed downstairs. She placed the newly found book about someone else's daughter on the kitchen counter.

Trying to forget her disappointment, Laven sat on the couch sketching something that had become etched in her mind. She held it back at arm's length to examine it.

Am I crazy? What am I doing to myself?

She ripped the page from the tablet and squeezed it into a ball and tossed it across the room. Hoping the next drawing would serve more of a purpose, the pencil started to shade a new page. After deciding she was at a point of inspection, she held the new sketch at arm's length. Yes, that's him.

As she added the finishing lines, she finally felt in control of something, even if it was only a number two graphite pencil. Lead wasn't used in pencils any longer.

She was laughing at herself for sounding like Jay when a knock on the door came.

Startled, she wondered if she should even answer it this late. After a moment a voice sounded.

"Laven, it's me Jay. Open the door."

Relieved, she rushed to the door.

"I thought you might be a little hungry so I brought some food from my favorite Mexican restaurant. I also brought you a few groceries and some other stuff."

My payback bill keeps growing.

"Thanks. How much do I owe you?"

"Don't worry about it." His smile appeared without a warning.

I am worried about it. This guy can't afford a decent car and he is spending money that he doesn't have. I won't be one of his biggest rushes and be someone that can't pay him back. I can and I will.

"Let's try these chimichangas before they get cold. The other groceries can wait a few minutes. Let's pray."

He really believes this stuff. She bowed with him.

"Do I have to quote scripture to eat it?" She tried to lessen the intensity of the last conversation.

"Not unless you are so inclined. No strings here." He grinned.

"This is good. Not as good as the Well Wishes, but good. Probably less expensive too."

"Sadly, no discount there. Except for it's Two for One Tuesday." He laughed as he reached for a nacho chip.

The exchange was pleasant. Laven decided she was glad he had come back. She felt comfortable being alone, but didn't much like her own company.

"I really appreciate the groceries. Thanks for picking them up. I will repay you. I promise. I will go find a place for them in the kitchen if there is space available around that box of cornflakes."

"While you are doing that, I will pick up our mess here so I won't have to leave a tip." he snickered.

Laven was loading the refrigerator when Jay's question turned her around to look.

"What is this?"

The blood surged to her face. He was holding a slightly wrinkled picture she had drawn.

"It looks like me, especially the smile! That is really good from memory."

Laven didn't know whether to run across the room to grab the drawing or run to the door. She did neither. She stood awkwardly wordless.

"I ahh... you were the last person I saw so I uhh."

"You said you weren't a good artist. You are very good!"

She had to change the subject. "Let me finish putting the groceries away and I will show you something."

"Oh, that last sack isn't groceries."

"What is it?" Laven looked in the white bag with startled amazement. It was filled with art supplies. There were various sizes of brushes, numerous tubes of oil paint, and small canvases.

She was speechless. It was probably the nicest thing she had ever received. But she would not look at it as a gift. She would give him his money back for this too.

"Wow! How thoughtful of you! How much do I owe

you?"

"Nothing."

"You paid nothing? What, did you do steal this stuff?" she smiled.

"A gift requires no pay back."

"Come in here and look at this."

Jay sat on the sofa and waited to see what Laven had to show him.

"This is him," she said as she handed Jay the tablet holding her last sketch.

"Him who?"

"The guy who rented me the car. I saw him mostly from the side view as he showed me where it was parked. Before that, I was busy filling out the paperwork."

Jay's eyebrows moved together and he put his free hand to his mouth. He pulled his cell phone from his pocket.

Who is he calling this late? I am not in the mood to

speak to the police.

"Look at this," he said as he put his phone to her face. "Seeing that the car was leaving the scene of your accident, I snapped a picture."

"It looks just like the guy that rented me the car! But you said that a female had been driving the car that hit me," Laven said.

"A female or someone with a wig disguised as one. We'll show this sketch to the police tomorrow. Earlier, I gave them a print out of the picture I took."

"I hope they get this figured out soon. I only took two weeks leave from work. I can't possibly tell my supervisor that I need to take off longer because of a pending police investigation and I can't have them calling me at work with questions. I just want this settled and my name cleared."

"What do you do?"

"I work for a utility company in the billing department. It's not my dream job, but it pays well and they provide health coverage and offer a retirement plan. It works for me." Laven thought of her small gray cubicle with walls that protect her from having to interact with anyone. Other employees with similar work spaces had their fabric covered partial walls bursting with photographs of family, vacations, and other memorabilia. Hers were unencumbered, plain, sterile, but private.

"Sounds like a good job, but not lending to your creativity. If you do something you love, it's not work."

"Have you heard of starving artists?"

"Good point! Vincent van Gogh sold only one painting while alive, Red Vineyard at Arles. He, like so many other masters, sadly perished in poverty."

"I will keep my day job. What about you? You have been helping me instead of showing real estate. "

"I don't require a lot of sleep. I do much of my work in the wee hours of the day."

Well, it's not working for you. Maybe if you got out and beat the bushes for customers when the sun was up, you could drive a car that didn't shoot like a western outlaw.

"I have been stealing a lot of your hours. Is there

anything I can do to help you catch up?"

"Don't be so loose with the word steal." He winked.

Laven winced, remembering that she was being looked at like a modern day outlaw.

"I didn't steal that car, Jay. Do you believe me?"

"I wouldn't be keeping company with you if I thought you had done something against the law."

I don't know why you were pestered with having to accompany me. First, it was an agreement with the physician to keep an eye on me and now it is the law enforcement. All I ever wanted to do was to fly beneath the radar."

"I am not "pestered" to watch over you, Laven. It is convenient not to have to come up with an excuse to be with you."

Laven's cheeks burned, giving her a natural blush.

"Can you remember anything else about the man at the airport?"

"Only that he wore winter gloves and it wasn't that cold outside."

"Did you notice that when he handed you the keys?"

"No, there were no keys. I noticed the gloves when I was signing the paperwork and when he pointed me to the car."

"No keys?"

"Right, he said the car was open and had a push to start button. It was the first time I had driven a car like that. I actually didn't even know that they had them."

"A remote ignition. Did he follow you to the car?"

"No, he just pointed it out and hurried off in another direction."

"The least he could have done is to help you with your luggage if he was going to frame you in a car heist."

It felt good to be believed. Now if he would only see that she was telling the truth about the rock with the warning on it.

A small corner of her mind hadn't totally released the suspicion that he had thrown the stone.

"I am overwhelmed by the gift of art supplies. Thank you so much!"

"Maybe you can re-gift me by returning some of the paint on a canvas in the form of a painting."

He did it again. Amazingly, his smile has the power to both send chills and melt me.

"Maybe. It was the nicest gift I ever received."

"It's really no big deal."

"To me, it's huge."

Jay stared at her. "Did you get gifts when you were a kid?"

"My mother sent no return address boxes of stuff. She didn't know me so she didn't know what I needed, like 'her' for instance. She sent expensive name brand clothes that only got me hated. I usually passed the stuff out to the rest of the kids."

Most of everything went to Sally Ella Rue for payment not to bully me.

"You don't like brand named items?"

"If I didn't have a name that meant anything, then why should I care about the name of some designer? Besides, for a girl who wanted to invisible and fly under the radar, wearing expensive clothes ran contrary to my objective."

"You may not have known the person who gave you the name, but it's yours now and you have made it beautiful. You don't have to be invisible anymore, Laven."

"Being invisible is safe. Just look what has happened to me when I stepped out of my comfort zone and was forced into visibility. Someone is trying to stone me and another is trying to frame me with a felony."

"I hate to burst your bubble, Laven, but someone as pretty as you can in no way be invisible. I suspect the reason that others have not tried harder to get to know you is that you are prickly, like a rose"

The pedals of a rose drop quickly but the thorny stem remains for years.

"It's getting late."

"I must have struck a cord, you are pushing back again."

No, you hit a thorn and there are plenty more where that one came from. If you were smart, you would push away from me."

"You, don't have to stand alone, Laven, you can lean on me.."

I have to save both of us.

"It's not so bad being alone. When you are alone you don't have to lean on anybody."

"You are going to push back and push back until you fall over. Who will be there to help you up?"

Something deep inside was yearning for him to stay, but the natural cover rose up with thorns.

"You should go now."

"You can throw me out, but I am not giving up on you."

"I need to get some sleep. "

"I put my number on speed dial. Press # 2 if you need me."

"Just out of curiosity, why did you select # 2?"

"Because I shouldn't be the first one that you call on when you need help."

"Who is # 1?"

"He is here with us now, but you told me earlier that you were fed up talking about Him." Jay smiled and looked upward. "Good night, Laven. Remember, lean in."

When the lock on the door clicked, Laven thought about the slip of paper that was wrapped around the chocolate candy from the Well Wishes restaurant. She wondered if they all said the same thing. She hadn't read Jay's yet.

Chapter 7

~~~

LAVEN HADN'T NOTICED THE small easel in the bag when she first saw the art supplies Jay had bought for her. It now held the canvas that was changing with each stroke. Art products are not cheap. She hoped that this painting would turn out nice to show how much she appreciated his gift to her.

A knock on the door startled Laven causing her to streak the line she was working on. Annoyed at the mess the knock had caused, she walked to the door.

The peek hole revealed a harmless looking lady holding a flat, white, shiny box so she slowly twisted the knob. Before the door was fully opened, a wild fury pushed through knocking Laven to the floor. A massive fleecy creature pounced excitedly around the room.

Laven jumped up, but not in time to save her wet canvas from hitting the floor. She cringed when the large paw smashed dead center onto the painting and shared paint blotches around the wood floor like stenciled paw prints.

Another knock at the door happened. Once again, she looked at the harmless looking lady standing on the front steps.

Before Laven could speak, the lady began. "I'm sorry, the door locked before I could stop her and, well, I guess she has already introduced herself. But let me make it more formal. This is Prism, your mother's poodle. Well, now your poodle."

"Poodle! This is a transfigured horse!!"

"Oh, and I am Lula and you are Laven?"

Laven nodded. "You knew my mother?"

"Yes, dear. She spoke of you often. She loved you very much."

The words rang hollow in her ears. "She had a strange way of showing it. This being the most recent example!" She pointed toward the large dog. "I don't want this animal! Could you please find another home for it. I don't live here so I wouldn't know where to start looking for a home for it."

"Oh, no darling. This girl was precious to your mother and she wanted you to have her. Here, I brought you a box of candy and I left a bag of dog food out in front. She has an allergy to corn so she needs to eat this very brand so as not to become ill."

"I don't want her! But thanks for the chocolates." As Laven walked toward the kitchen, the big dog named Prism goosed her with her snout. "Stop!" she commanded as she placed the chocolates in the cabinet with glass door.

"Oh, she does that, but she is a good girl. You will love her when you get to know her."

"She is getting to know me a little too intimately. I don't want her." She looked directly at the bearer of her living inheritance. Laven noted that she must have put her make up on in the dark with her eyes closed and her hands behind her back. Poor thing.

It looked as though she put colors on a palate and rubbed her face on it.

She had a heavy build except for her thin arms and legs making her appear to be a tomato with sticks for arms and legs. She wouldn't have been able to pull this look off in a comic book. She wore white gloves and she must not use her hands much because the white glove treatment had passed the clean test.

"Like I said, to know her is to love her."

"Like I said, I don't want this curly white plague. Stop licking me!"

"She is a standard poodle, but considerably larger than most."

"This is not a dog. It's a horse! Get off of me!"

Lula laughed. "You have to be careful. She thinks she is a lap dog."

"Get off of me! I don't like you

"It looks like she loves you."

"The feeling is not reciprocated. Of all the cute dogs

in the world she had to choose you and then plague me. You are a wooly horse. I'll find you a new home tomorrow."

"Funny you should call her a horse. She eats like one. Like I said, her food is out in front. It's quite expensive, but the only brand found that she doesn't have a bad reaction to."

"Please tell me she is house broken. She probably does other things like a horse."

"Well…"

"I am getting nervous, what?"

"Well, she is housebroken, but in a non-traditional way.."

"What does that mean?"

"She's trained to go in the house."

"Then, she is not house broken. The whole premise is that you teach the dog to do their business outdoors."

"Prism has been taught to show you when she needs to go outside. However, if she is home alone, she has been trained to go in the bathroom."

"She goes on the toilet?"

"Not exactly. She goes in the shower."

"Okay, that is disgusting! It's not happening!"

"When you return, you use tissue to flush the solid waste. There is a long handled brush and cleansing agents to disinfect the shower floor."

"My Mother continues to torment me from beyond."

"Prism is loveable and a good watchdog. She doesn't like strangers. She is very smart. She is a good girl. She can open the shower door; in fact she can open most doors. She can open the back door but knows she can't get back in. She's alert and trainable and very instinctive. She will grow on yo

"I just hope that she doesn't grow!" At that, Prism began to lick Laven's face. "I don't like you."

"Well, I must go now."

"Oh, please don't leave yet. I have more to ask you about my mother."

"I apologize, but I don't have the time at the moment. But here." She extended her gloved hand toward Laven.

"What is this?"

"It is the key to the garage in the rear of the house. Your mother kindly allowed me to store my car there. Please feel free to drive it while you are here. The keys to the ignition are under the flowerpot by the entrance to the garage. Please return both sets of keys there upon your departure."

Being directed to a car. This feels like Deja Vu. Gloves, what was it about gloves in this place?

It felt too much like the airport experience for Laven's comfort. She stared at Lula's white gloves. One finger on the right hand seemed to be limp and empty.

Lula turned abruptly and headed for the door. "Enjoy your beautiful Prism. I will miss her company. And oh, dear Laven, never, never sell the bed. Have it shipped and take your new pet and leave this town immediately."

"But, why? Will I see you again? I have so many

questions about my mother."

"Perhaps we will meet again, just not here. You must leave Rising Falls as soon as possible. I must run now." She finished and the door locked behind her.

Prism jumped up and placed her paws on Laven's shoulders.

"Stop it! I don't want paws painted on my sweater! You have already ruined my painting! You are not going to ruin my life! I will look for a new home for you tomorrow!"

Prism answered her with a lick across the face.

"Stop it! I don't like you!"

She ran to the door and stood on her hind legs bracing herself with her front paws as though trying to look out the peek hole.

"Now you miss Lula. Why didn't you do this when

she was here and then leave with her?"

Prism began to jump at the door.

"Are you trying to tell me something? Are you dancing to go out?"

Laven started to the door when a recording of Jay's words sounded in her memory. "If you go outside and the door closes, you had better have a key or you aren't getting back in." She dropped the house key into her sweater pocket and it made a clinking sound when it hit those that Lula had given her. The picture of the glove with the floppy pinky finger flashed in her mind.

How does she expect to meet again if she told me to leave town? She left no way for me to contact her.

Prism burst out the door with as much velocity as she had entered and validated the reason for the dance.

She kicked the fallen leaves with her hind feet and then after a couple of circles shot toward the rear of the house.

Trying to keep up, Laven nearly tripped over the oversized bag of dog food.

"Prism!" Laven called as the mammoth fluffy mass grew smaller the farther away she traveled.

She noticed the detached garage that looked more like a cottage and was curious to glance in at Lula's car. Was it a Volkswagen, a Minnie Cooper or perhaps a Volvo station wagon? It would have to wait. Her living inheritance was leaving her sight.

Would it be so bad if she ran away and someone found her? Maybe someone would like her. I don't.

Laven called again a bit more softly, but continued to follow her into a thicket of trees.

She finally caught up with Prism playing by a small spring that had created a pond.

"Thanks for leading me here. It's pretty. I like it."

Prism ran to her and began to lick her hand.

"I said I like this place. I still don't like you, not at all!"

Laven sat on a flat-topped rock that nature seemed to have intended for a chair. Red and yellow leaves were taking turns twirling down to join the crunchy ones that had preceded them. Small wild flowers bravely showed their blossoms not seeming to care about the changing season.

Across the pond was a fence, not placed there by nature. The crisscrossing bars held tightly together enclosing what looked like a ten-foot square area. A fancy gate that appeared to be locked finished the four-sided enclosure.

Perhaps it was meant for a garden and the decorative metal work was there to keep out animals that might otherwise invite themselves to dinner.

Laven wanted to take a closer look at the fenced off portion, but Prism had other plans as she headed back in the direction of the house.

She walked beside her on the return trip.

"You were excited to show me that place weren't you? Did my mother walk you there often?"

Prism's tongue stuck out as she panted happily.

"I'll take that as a yes." As she looked, the abundance of white curls reflecting the colors of fall gave Laven an understanding of why her name was chosen. This understanding in no way changed the fact that she disliked the mammoth animal.

Up ahead, stood a wreck of a car that seemed to worsen with each day.

Prism sprinted excitedly up to Jay and liberally shared her kisses.

Hmm. I thought she didn't like strangers. Some watchdog she is.

Maybe all these strange characters were playing her. She looked forward to the day she could put this place behind her.

"Whooa! This is one big poodle!"

"Are you sure? I was thinking it was either two poodles walking closely together or a horse in disguise."

"Where did he come from?"

"He is a she. And she was one of my mother's farewell gifts to me."

Jay laughed as he rubbed the unclipped fur.

"Could you find a home for her?"

"I think your mother already did."

"I don't want her!"

"Aww, look, you are going to hurt her feelings and give her a complex."

Laven's thoughts traveled back in time to the orphanage.

"Nobody wants you," the girl named Sally Ella Rue mocked her on more occasions than she wanted to remember. "Your mother doesn't even want you. She threw you away. I don't have parents but you do have a mother and she doesn't want you."

"I was beginning to wonder where you were when you didn't answer the door or your phone." Jay brought her back to the present.

"Prism took me for a walk."

"Prism?"

"That's the name of the horse that resembles a dog. I'm serious about looking for a home for her. Do you know anyone who you think would take her?"

"You might learn to like her."

"It won't happen. My mother made provisions for the other unwanted gift, but I am told this one eats like a horse and she requires some kind of gourmet dog food."

"I saw the 80lb. bag over there."

80lbs? I wonder how Lula managed that out of her vehicle. I didn't even look to see what she was driving. Hmm, Two cars for one funny little lady.

"Speaking of food, I thought we might break out some of the human variety and build a couple of sandwiches. "

"I thought there were no strings attached to the groceries you brought." Laven smiled.

"I'd be glad to quote some scripture as payment."

"I'll reward you with food if you don't!"

She pulled out a handful of keys as she spoke.

"You have as many keys there as a building manager."

"Lula said I could use her car while I am here

"Lula?"

"She's the lady who dropped this four legged monster off."

"That was nice of her, but you might want to check the registration before you drive it."

He joked but she took it as some seriously wise advise. After what she had been through, a second stolen vehicle could move her from being a suspect to being an inmate.

"I'll do that! And I will wear gloves. Everyone else does around here. I should just start wearing gloves all the time and keep my finger prints to myself."

"You might want to keep a muzzle on your furry friend ,the way she shadows you."

Laven's questioning stare needed no words as they stepped inside the door.

"A dog's nose print is as unique as our finger prints.

Some breeders use them as positive identification. The prints from that black nose could place you at the scene." Jay grinned.

Laven did not. "That is even more of a reason to find her a new home. I don't need a canine to frame me. There is already a human doing that." Laven wondered if she was being watched.

Chapter 8

~~~

SHE SAT UP IN BED and stretched. The conversation was light and happy with Jay the night before. No preaching and nothing from the font with the exception of the unsolicited information about the first recorded sandwich being invented by some Rabbi and not by the Earl of Sandwich.

Then the weight of reality hit. When was she going to be able to leave this place?

Was the threat on her life real or just a mean prank? The longer she stayed, the more danger she was in and the biggest danger of all was the softening of her armor toward Jay. This feeling can't grow. It can't last. *It would not take long for him to find that all I have to share is my inner nothingness*.

Not wanting to depend on Jay any longer for

transportation, she decided to take Lula up on her offer to use her car. She showered and dressed in record time and hurried to the garage and peeked inside to see what she would be driving. She was taken aback to see what the amusing little lady drove. It was a black Mercedes hardtop convertible so shiny she could see her reflection. She found it impossible to imagine Lula driving this vehicle. She couldn't imagine herself driving this vehicle. It was definitely not what someone trying not to draw attention to themselves would choose to drive, but if she wished to be independent of Jay she had no choice.

She remembered his advice to check the registration before driving it so she covered her fingerprints with her sweater sleeve and opened the door with the key Lula had loaned her and looked in the glove compartment.

The vehicle was indeed registered to Lula Higgins. It looked legal and in order, so she walked around and climbed into the driver's seat.

When she turned on the ignition she noticed the gas gauge pointed to empty. That would be her first destination as she backed out of the garage.

She didn't feel far from the ground in this sleek sports car as she drove down Chequered Lane and turned at the intersection that led into town.

She pulled into the first gas station she spotted and had to reposition the vehicle because the gas tank was on the opposite side as of that of her own car.

As she was filling the tank, her eye caught a stunningly gorgeous lady with a luxurious head of thick, shining hair. It seemed to swing in slow motion like a hair product commercial and the well-trained soft curls fell perfectly back into place.

Her tall slender frame seemed to be perfectly proportioned. The clothes she wore accentuated all her positive attributes. She was 'beauty contestant winner' beautiful and her long legs ended at what were obviously designer shoes.

She is staring.

Her beauty would make it impossible for anyone to see Laven. But if she was invisible, why then was this dark haired beauty staring at her? She looked away quickly to erase any idea that she had been staring back.

"Hello." The flawless looking lady spoke showing teeth so perfect and white that they had to have been cosmetically enhanced and must have cost a fortune.

"Hi." Laven focused on filling the tank of the sports car.

"Nice car."

"Yeah, it's not mine." Laven answered hoping this would end the conversation. A car like this brought her out from under the radar.

"I didn't think so." The lady returned in a snarky tone

Laven noticed that the beauty she had seen came to an abrupt stop. All she saw now was rude and the rudeness deserved no response.

"I think I saw you at the diner with my ex."

"Your axe?" Her accent confused Laven.

"No, my ex-fiancé!" she said with a curt attitude.

"You mean the Well Wishes?"

"That's no diner, honey. I saw the two of you at the Sip and Chew. Just a warning, sweetheart, he's not what he appears to be. He'll drag you along with his razzle-dazzle rhetoric and then drop you like a hot potato. You're better off cutting it off before he cuts you off."

"Are you talking about Jay Shane?"

"Seriously? Is that the name he gave you!?" She kept laughing as she pulled her long legs into her car. "Tell him you talked to Mercedes Diaz." She called out as she sped away.

The screeching of the tires told Laven that Mercedes was not over Jay. Next to the nuclear bomb, there is no greater explosion than that let off by an old flame. Laven wanted no part of it. Her thoughts traveled back in time.

Sally Ella Rue was a tall, willowy girl with blond hair clipped at her jaw line. She was as agile as a cat. She could jump fences on a single bound, climb any tree and land on the top bunk as if it were the bottom one. She had fallen madly in love with Micah Hinsley. He had a crush on Laven and followed her around like a puppy. He was a nice boy, but Laven only thought of him as her new foster brother. Micah and Laven left the foster home at the same time. Sally Ella thought they had left together, but nothing could have been farther from the truth.

The state paid for him to attend the university, but because Laven had a mother, her profile didn't meet the criteria, therefore; she worked her way through junior college.

Word had traveled to Laven that Sally Ella hated her, but that wasn't breaking news. That was historical, dating back to when they were five years old. After graduation, she never heard from any of the foster kids again.

As Laven watched the car speed off, she decided there was nothing pretty about this physically attractive person. She wasn't worth the 1.7 ounce tube of dark brown oil paint it would take to paint her hair.

~

She pulled the car filled with gas back into the garage and walked into the house thinking about the exchange she had had with the dark haired rude person.

She needn't worry about cutting it off with Jay. Nothing has started with him and it will remain that way. There is absolutely nothing to cut.

She walked to the house thinking about how trust is food for the foolish. Never again would she allow herself to be disappointed by trusting.

Prism welcomed her home with organic solid matter on the shower floor.

"You are so not going home with me! I don't like you!"

She started to bark excitedly which was an indication that a knock was about to happen on the door. Laven finished sanitizing the shower and went downstairs.

Just like clock work there was a knock on the door.

Jay's face showed through the peek hole.

He was carrying a bag of Chinese take out food.

"Because you come bearing food, I will let you enter." Laven said.

Jay prayed before they ate. Laven couldn't help think about the rude lady's warning. He isn't what he appears to be.

They silently ate the packaged Oriental food. Laven finally broke the silence.

"I took Lula's car out today. It was registered to her so I didn't have to hide my finger prints."

"Really? What kind is it? He asked as he picked at the chicken chow mien with his chopsticks.

"Ironically, it is a shiny black Mercedes convertible."

"Ha. Not the make I would have expected, but irony?"

"The irony is that when I pulled the black, shiny Mercedes into the gas station, I encountered a dark shiny haired Mercedes."

Jay stared at her for a moment and then said, "I'm sorry."

"Sorry? Why are you sorry?"

I wonder if he had told her that her name reminded him of an exotic sports car?

"She's probably not the nicest person you would want to encounter."

"She said that you weren't the nicest person either. She said you are not who you say you are."

"It's more like I'm not who she wanted me to be. She was after a landed man."

"Landed man?"

"A man who owns much land."

She may be beautiful, but not very intuitive not to notice that he is broke as a joke.

"She said the two of you were engaged to be married."

"That was her goal not mine."

"She's very beautiful."

"That she is and she has the bills for cosmetic procedures to prove it. She had me fooled, but it didn't take long to figure out that the beauty stopped quickly and had no depth beyond the make-up."

It wouldn't take Sherlock Holmes to deduct that.

"Right at first I thought she might be the one. Thank God for the 11 carat diamond alarm."

"What was that about?"

"It was about God showing me who she really was. She took me into a jewelry store and showed me the ring she wanted. There had been no mention of marriage and after I saw the price tag of 35 Grand, there never was. She had a bit of a fit when I told her I couldn't afford something that extravagant."

I don't know what he traded for this car but if it was an upgrade, it should have been her first clue that a giant diamond wasn't happening.

"She definitely wasn't the one, but she did me the favor of showing me what I didn't want in a wife."

"I didn't find her very nice either."

Jay stared at her with a look that froze her into a statue.

"Laven, I have something to…..

Prism growled and then broke into a full-fledged bark. His sentence ended with a rap at the door.

Laven wrestled around the big dog and opened the door. She asked the familiar officers to come inside.

"Did you learn who stole the vehicle?"

"The license was from another vehicle and the VIN number was gone. There were no fingerprints other than yours.

"Because he wore gloves; I told you!"

"No, you told me." Jay corrected and then unfolded a slightly wrinkled paper that he pulled from his pocket. Laven sketched this rendering of the man who rented her the car. Compare it to the one I took with my phone. This is the person you need to be speaking to."

Barely glancing, the officer handed Laven's picture to his counterpart who placed it in a file. "We will run a facial recognition on it."

"There is something else."

"What?" Laven worried that it was something to do with Lula's car even though the registration had checked out.

"An OBD was found in the wrecked vehicle," the officer announced.

"A what?" Laven asked.

Jay stepped forward. "An Onboard Diagnostic. It's a hand held device for programming keys in immobilizer units on vehicles."

"It had yours and only your fingerprints all over it."

"Well, no one told me to wear gloves like everyone else does here."

"Did you see this device?" The other policeman produced a picture of a tiny instrument.

"Yes, I saw that and thought it was a garage opener or something and placed it under the driver's seat. I was in a hurry to get to my dying mother's bedside."

Saying this made her remember her mother's last words or lack there of.

Jay spoke. "Are you sure that isn't a code grabber

that uses an electronic pulse to replay codes?'

"That is irrelevant. Either is a mechanism to enter without a key. In this case, it wasn't the vehicle's owner who operated the device."

"We may have additional questions to ask you while we continue the investigation."

I can't have this following me back. I can't have them calling my workstation with questions. How can I explain to my supervisor that I may be a suspect in a felony?

"How much longer?"

"We will try to expedite the procedure, Miss Hoddy. We appreciate your cooperation.

"Did you interview the neighbors?"

"We did try, but that house has been vacant for over a year."

"I saw a light in the window one night and the curtain move the next day. There is someone in that house."

Jay spoke again. "Look, she has been through a lot.

The man had gloves on. It appears that an effort was made to clear the car of any fingerprints.

Of course hers are the only ones you'll find, but why would she get directly off the plane and steal a car? She has no idea what an OBD is."

"Don't forget the rock! Someone might be trying to kill me and I am the person you are questioning?"

"We will continue to survey the area. Please call us immediately if you have any information. We will be in contact and try to get this resolved as soon as possible."

"Nice drawing," the other policeman added as they walked out the door.

The blue uniforms left but the white headache began to bark.

"I'll bet she is hungry. She already finished off the small bag of dog food."

"I'll bring in the dog food, if you'll keep the door open for me."

Laven followed the bag, Jay, and the barking, giant dog into the kitchen.

"Where do you want this?"

"In this closet would be a nice place, but I'll have to get all these old magazines out first."

Jay sat the dog food down and they began to pull tall stacks of magazines of every imaginable subject out onto the kitchen floor.

"Do you want any of these?"

"No, they look pretty old, but not old enough to have increased in value.

"I'll take them out to the garbage."

"That will be great," Laven said as her sight rested on one of the mailing label address stickers. Lula Higgins, 6336 Chequered Lane.

Had Lula lived here with her mother? She had no information on how to contact the strange little lady who had much needed answers to a myriad of questions.

After the last trip out to the garbage bin, Jay opened the re-sealing bag and slid it into the now empty closet.

Laven turned to Jay. "Thank you so much!"

"No big deal. It's funny what old ladies hold on to."

"Oh, not that. Thanks for taking those out too, but mostly thank you for believing I didn't steal that car."

Jay smiled. "Shall we see if our Chinese food remains edible? If not the Sip and Chew awaits us."

Laven wondered if she could recapture the moment when he was about to tell her something

Chapter 9

~~~

"WOULD YOU BE STILL?" The only thing worse than a hyper dog running up and down the stairs is a gigantic, hyper dog running up and down the stairs."

Prism jumped up on the bed.

"Get down! We have nothing in common. Well, except the fact that neither of us is wanted here."

Laven climbed out of bed and into the shower, but not before she scrubbed it with the disinfecting cleanser.

The hot pulsating water massaged her scalp. She wished it could wash away her past and make her whole and new; but no matter how hard she scrubbed, all the hurts of what was before still remained. She made a promise to herself not let the pain compound in this place.

She inhaled the fragrance of her lotion. It had a fresh flowery scent that lifted her spirits. She pulled her hair into a ponytail, donned her jeans, a comfortable top along with a protective attitude and prepared herself for whatever was to come. Hopefully, today she would get word from the police that she had been exonerated and this place would become a faded page in her history.

The knock on the front door could barely be heard over Prism's loud barking.

"Okay, Okay!" Laven ran down the stairs barefoot. She couldn't get to the peek hole to see who was outside because of the furry mass that blocked the door.

"It's just me, Laven," came Jay's voice through the barks.

"Sorry! Prism is blocking the door." She called as she tried to wrestle 'the horse with a perm' out of the way.

Finally, she was able to reach around the overgrown beast and twist the knob.

"Good morning! I have free tickets for a serious

153

adventure."

"If you haven't noticed, I already have an adventure wrapped in poodle cloth.

"Feeling gutsy? I'll take that 'deer in the headlights look' as a definite yeah! Let's go!"

"I uh, can't leave my furry inheritance. Have you found a home for her yet?"

"No, but she'll survive while you are gone."

"I'm not worried about her survival. I'm concerned that nothing else will survive here.

"Nonsense! She'll be fine."

"Maybe, but I'm certain that she will have her own serious adventure here alone and it won't be pretty."

"What could she hurt?"

"I'm afraid to imagine."

"Close her in the bedroom. She'll use the shower." He smiled.

"Yuk! Don't remind me."

"Come on. You'll love it!'

"I don't believe there is a drawer or door she can't open around here. And she can jump like nobody's business. She managed to get my purse off of a six foot high bureau."

"Take your purse. What else can she hurt? Look, she knows we are leaving her."

"Prism, come upstairs with me. And no I don't like you." She looked back at Jay. "Let me change and I will be right back."

"You are perfect. Come as you are. Well, maybe grab some shoes while I take Prism out and give the shower floor a break."

Laven frowned disgustedly. "What shoes do I need to wear?"

"Probably not the white squirrels, but tennis shoes will work."

I hope he doesn't want to play tennis. Not one of my bones is athletic.

Laven braced herself, but the rickety car spared her of any loud bangs.

"Did you fix the gun noise?"

"No, not yet."

"Remember, Lula offered her car if you had rather drive that."

"What would you prefer?"

"I'm content with ole Patch." She rubbed the dash.

Jay had an approving look on his face.

For some reason he likes this hunk of junk.

"You have given her a name." His smile out-shined the sun.

"I still consider that very generous of her to offer you her car."

"I thought so too. She is a little strange but a lot nice. I hope she comes back so I can ask her some questions, but if I had dropped that creature off, the person who took her would never see me again. Have you had a chance to look for a new home for her?"

Jay laughed. "I think you already asked me that. So

you want me to be that person who does the drive by dogging. I see."

"No one would take her from me because I couldn't think of one thing nice to say about her."

Jay turned the volume up on the radio. "I like this song. It's one of my favorites. I am so glad the radio works."

I wonder if it truly works. It is always only on this station. Maybe it is stuck.

"You really enjoy Christian music, don't you?

"Is there another kind?" He grinned. "It's all about the messaging in any genre."

"Hey, there is my friend Scott!"

Laven looked but saw no one. "Where?"

"There on air. He is not only a talented broadcaster, he's the genuine article, the real deal!"

"Where are we going?"

"He walks his talk."

"Umm, Where are we going?"

"You'll see soon."

"So you have free tickets?" She asked to ensure he wasn't spending money that he didn't have.

"Well, I know the pilot."

"We're going on a flight?"

"Yes and then some."

As they left town, the car began to sputter.

"Is it going to stall?"

"No, it's just missing."

Boy, is it ever missing!

She glanced around the interior. The list was too long to think.

"Missing what?"

"Bad plugs. I need to replace them. Or it could be the coil."

The ride was bumpy so Laven sighed in relief when they pulled up to a modernistic building that appeared to have a space capsule sitting on the roof.

"Here we are. Better take your purse."

"I thought you said it was free."

Jay laughed. "I'm just not sure ole Patch's locks can be trusted. There are lockers inside.

Laven wasn't going to mention it, but he was about to park in a reserved spot. Hopefully, the pilot had given him permission. The last thing he needed was a parking ticket.

A long black van was pulling out as Jay was steering ole Patch into the vacant parking spot. The windows in the van were covered with a dark tint that was nearly opaque. Laven could barely make out a young girl's face inside the black window. She waved at Laven. Laven smiled and waved back, but the girl who looked to be in her late teens or early twenties kept her hand on the window as the van left the airport parking lot. Was the girl just resting her out -stretched fingers on the glass or was she reaching out to Laven?

She remembered holding her hand on the orphanage window when she was little and it wasn't to say goodbye. There was a pen and paper in Jay's cracked console that Laven used them to jot down the van's license plate number.

"What's that?"

"There was something unsettling about that girl."

"Like what?"

"I stopped waving, but I never saw her hand leave the window."

"Are you ready?" Jay smiled and placed the note pad in his pocket.

"Should I not have written on that?"

"It's fine," he answered as he worked to open the jammed door.

The building felt clean with live plants enjoying the sunlight spilling through the large windows.

"Here, put this on?"

Laven looked around. Several men were standing near them wearing the same uniforms. Others stood in street clothes. Jay seemed to recognize one of them and smiled, but the man ignored the smile and quickly turned away.

"Where is the dressing room?" She tried to break the discomfort from the moment.

"You don't need a dressing room, but you might want to visit the restroom first. I'll wait here with your suit."

Laven watched Jay from a distance. He was handing a man something. It was probably the free tickets. The other man stared at what Jay had given him and hurried off. Perhaps he was confirming that the date on the ticket hadn't expired.

She returned with a decision. "Although, I don't mind looking like the team, I think I'll just wear what I have on." Days of having to dress like everyone else gave Laven an aversion to uniforms.

Jay grinned. "No, you have to wear Nomex."

"What is that? Any relation to Versace ?"

Jay laughed. "It's an anti -static fabric with heat and flame resistant properties for added protection." Jay knelt on the floor and unfolded the suit. "Put your leg in here."

Laven obeyed, ignoring his warm touch.

"All this for a sight seeing flight?"

"We are actually going to sky dive."

Laven swallowed hard. "As in high dive into the air out of a plane?"

"Do you want to go?"

As he stood to zip her suit, she searched through a mental catalog of excuses to use to say no.

In the end, she muttered, "Just as well."

He looked deep into her eyes like he had something to say to her. His concentrating stare made her feel uncomfortable.

"If we stand here too long, I might have a change of mind."

"Okay, which of your six pockets do you want to hold your locker key?"

"This one I guess." He snapped the key securely into the pocket, tightened the Velcro belt and handed her some goggle type glasses that matched the ones he carried.

"Ready?"

"As ready as I am going to get."

"Let's go." He motioned for two of the standing men to follow.

The man who had ignored him earlier seemed to give him a look of acknowledgement.

He politely introduced Laven to her flight fellows and led her to the rear of the compact plane on what would be her maiden voyage in an aircraft this small and her very first time she would jump out of one. Probably the last, if she survived this one.

She peered out the window at the town below.

Jay pointed out several points of interest and then he told the pilots to circle around the house beneath them. "It's your mother's house."

"Look, Jay! That's the little pond behind it. You can only see parts of it through the trees. There is a metal fence but the foliage is blocking it from sight. He nodded, obviously not as excited as she was to see it.

The plane picked up speed and began to climb higher and higher.

The sky was clear and you could see forever and yet nothing at all. Cars, even houses grew smaller until they were too tiny to spot. The next thing she knew, the side door was open and Jay was guiding her toward it. Actually, he was gently pushing her toward it. "Sit down." Her legs swung out into the sky and took her breath away. How thankful she was that she had visited that   restroom. He helped her place the goggles over her eyes.

"Are you okay?"

"I'm not feeling so gutsy now. My guts are climbing up to my throat."

"Relax and be glad we aren't doing this in Florida on a Sunday."

"Why?"

"Because it's against the law for an unmarried woman to parachute there on Sundays."

Could you put a lid on your font? I am about to

commit suicide by air.

Sitting on the edge of the opening in the plane was robbing her of her breath. This was against logic. Everything within her screamed, don't do this!

"How far away from the earth are we?"

"Over two miles."

Laven sucked in some sky. Heaven must be on the next level up. Every fiber of her body was resisting leaving the security of the plane. There was nothing to catch her, but everything has to end somewhere. She hoped that the ending today wouldn't be her life as pathetic as it was.

This was infinitely more frightening than her first time off the high dive. Water was there to break her fall. Nothing she could see from here would break her fall. Would she just break?

"Changing your mind? Having second thoughts?"

"I am on my forty second thought."

"Do you trust me?"

"You have done this before, right?"

"A couple of times." He smiled, but she was too shaky to enjoy it.

"You know when to pull the cord, right?"

"Trust me, Laven."

If she ever had a reason to pray, this was it. She said it all in one word, "GOD!"

"Now?"

"Just as well."

He squeezed her shoulder and positioned the tandem straps and pushed away from the plane. "Let's take a leap and rule the sky! "

She wanted to scream but she was too busy sucking in air. The blood rushed to her fingertips and the pressure pulled at her cheeks.

Suddenly they were free falling to the earth at 120 miles per hour. She had an intense adrenaline rush. It was exhilarating and like nothing she had ever experienced. It was the most elating thrill of her dull life.

This is what dying must feel like.

Airborne, she felt like she was being born into a new dimension. In Heaven, after we shed our earth-suits, will we be able to fly? she wondered. It was the most free she had ever felt.

It wasn't until Jay pulled the cord and she felt the jerk of the chute opening that she remembered he was behind her.

It didn't feel quite as free but it did feel safer. Now, instead of flying, they were floating. She took in the amazing views like she was breathing with her eyes.

What a vantage point. If God really was up there and He really cared about each of us, it was humanly impossible to even fathom his enormity.

Chapter 10

~~~

THAT HAD BEEN THE adventure of her life, right down to the landing. It wasn't until the parachute hit the ground behind them that Laven realized Jay's arms were embracing her. She looked over her shoulder pulled forward to break from his hold as they both stood to their feet. Firmly planted on terra firma, there was no need to trust anymore. She was in one piece and unbroken- on the outside anyway.

The drive to the house was a relatively quick one. Laven mentally re-experienced each phase of the jump.

She cataloged them in her memory. The side of her brain that captured good memories was nearly empty so she wanted to make sure she forgot nothing of this day.

She waved good-bye to Jay and insisted on letting herself into the house.

Once inside, she decided to surprise Jay with some of her delicious cheese soup tonight. She hummed when she added ingredients to the grated cheese and placed the combination in a pan on top of the gas stove.

Listen to me! Now he has me humming to his favorite song on the one station he listens to.

She stood at the bottom of the stairs and made a mental note to check the soup in about fifteen minutes.

Now was the moment of reckoning. She was about to find out what kind of adventure the furry furor had experienced.

She opened the bedroom door and, at once, saw that it had been an exciting one for Prism, too. The big dog didn't run to greet Laven, but sat nervously in the corner showing her teeth in what appeared to be an hilarious human- like smile.

"Bad girl!" Laven said, fighting back the urge to laugh.

The bed was stripped to the mattress. Drawers were opened and the contents scattered on the floor. One white slipper was nothing more than a pile of fibers.

"Cinderella is down to one slipper, but no happy ending will happen here."

The only upside to the situation was that there was no solid waste on the shower floor. To make sure it remained that way, she addressed the huge dog.

"Come on, Prism, let's get your destructive self outside."

Downstairs, Laven was about to open the door, but Prism stood stubbornly and barked.

"Come!" Laven commanded.

As if frustrated, Prism grabbed Laven's purse by the strap and brought it to her.

Laven stood dumbfounded and a little scared at the dog's intelligence. "Lula wasn't kidding when she said you were smart. You remembered that we couldn't get back in the house without the keys in my purse. Okay, you've redeemed yourself a little for the mess you made."

Laven's respect for the animal had grown but so had the desire to find her a new home. She decided her fear of commitment didn't stop at humans.

Still a little shocked, she followed Prism out in the yard and watched her kick at the dry leaves and run in circles. When she started for the back of the house, Laven called to her.

"No! You don't deserve to go to the pond today after the grand mess you left for me to clean up. Come!"

The front door key fit this lock as well. She wondered who if anyone else had a key that matched this one. They entered the side entrance by what once was a flower garden.

When she opened the bedroom door and had a second look, she decided she genuinely didn't like the whopper of a dog.

"You are a curse! I will not play maid to a mega poodle for the remainder of one of our lives. You are not worth the extra work! I wonder where a person can return a gift to someone who is no longer here?"

Laven began by gathering the remains of what once was a comfy slipper. She continued the task of picking up the articles that had been strewn across the floor and returned each to an assigned drawer.

She shook the bedding and stretched the sheets across the mattress. Laven stared at her brass inheritance. Her eyes went to the round jewel like glass in the center of the headboard. It was surrounded by a lighter color of metal than the rest of the bed. She climbed up on the fluffy duvet and traced around the frame of the glass. Her fingertips caught on a screw with threaded flat end, probably a bolt.

Oh no, something is missing. I wonder what?

The glass was concave. How interesting. She placed

her hand behind the glass and her hand appeared larger.

A magnifying glass!

She remembered her mother's parting words. Why put a magnifying glass in a headboard? A closer look at what, or was the bed a hiding place?

She followed the curve of the frame to see how it was attached. There were four small braces securing it to the bed frame, each was held with a tiny brass screw.

Where would she find a screwdriver small enough to fit in the slit on the top? She first tried a nail file, but even that was too thick. She searched the bathroom drawers and found a razor blade.

The corner of the blade did the trick. She carefully twisted each screw until

the framed glass was in her hand.

It was a magnifying glass without a handle. She searched around the brass bed to see if one might be hiding in the swirls. She took a closer look at the small post in the middle, the more important looking one that was different than the three on either side.

It was that lighter tone of metal like the frame of the glass. She worked on it for more than an hour, broke the corner of the blade and cut her finger before she found and loosened the last screw.

This not only looked more important. It was much more complicated. The three columns swung on hinges. The cylinders appeared as though the tops could be removed. After unsuccessfully twisting them off, Laven pushed the three together forming a perfect handle.

Once in place, a small opening appeared at the top. She took the framed glass and placed the threaded protruding bolt into the hole and twisted the two pieces tightly together.

Voila! The magnifying glass! Now to find the meaning, why did it merit my mother's passing words?

The sight of the ornate piece left her motionless. She looked at the intricately designed piece in her hand and her memory was pulled back to the hospital bed and the weak final spoken words. "Magnifying glass, bed, J…"

Time moved but Laven did not. She sat staring at the aged magnifying glass. What was it about this round glass framed with gold –toned, designed metal? She traced her finger around and around the metal frame trying to make sense of it all.

A magnifying glass -she was holding her mother's final sentiments in her hand.

This was it? This is what years of silence were saved for, a seemingly meaningless inanimate object.

She held it to the light as if the glass would provide a vision of her mother explaining everything. Nothing appeared but a close -up look at the wood grain in the slightly opened shutters.

She widened the gap of the wooden slats and looked outside. As she stared out, she felt like the six-year-old girl watching and waiting at the window, expecting her mother to come and rescue her, to pick her up and hold her in her arms. The pain and disappointment hadn't lessened but had grown with each year.

The taunting from the other girls led by Sally Ella Rue telling her to stop watching, that her mother would never come because she didn't want her. Laven had desired more than anything to prove them wrong. She yearned for her mother to rescue her, to tell her she was a good girl and that she loved her. Her mother never came. There were no comforting hugs, no words of encouragement. There was no one to put ribbons in her hair and tell her she was pretty. There was no one there to praise her for doing a good job. Laven caught all the hurtful mocks and tucked them away deep inside.

Now as an adult, all she had of her mother was a bed that wouldn't fit in her apartment, a dog she didn't want, and an old magnifying glass. The girls at the orphanage had been right. Laven added this to her internal pile of hurts.

Should she share with Jay what she had found? It was pretty like a piece of jewelry with curly cues of tarnished metal winding around it. It had an interesting ornamental handle but like the bed and the dog, it was nothing important.

She played back her mother's struggling words, "Magnifying glass, bed, J..."

The bed and magnifying glass were here but what about the J sound? Did she know Jay? Was she trying to warn her about him?

No, it was the soft G sound. Maybe she was going to add giant dog before she left.

Laven decided that Jay's font of useless information might provide something useful on the magnifying glass. She would show him.

All at once an alarm went off.

"The soup! It's the fire alarm! I forgot about the soup!"

Laven left Prism in the bedroom and with magnifying glass in hand ran down the stairs and into a cloud of smoke. Laven held her sleeve over her face with one hand and used the antique magnifying glass as a fan with the other, making her way through the thick gray mass.

She quickly removed the burning pan and turned off the burner. She flipped the exhaust fan switch, but it proved to be no match for the smoke in the room. She made her way to the window and opened it. The air was beginning to clear as she reached for different objects with which to hold the window open. She saw the scrapbook she had found on the counter, but it was not substantial enough to hold it open so she just slid the magnifying glass inside it for safe keeping. She spotted the flat white box of chocolates, made her way across the room, opened the glass door and reached for the cellophane covered box.

It fit perfectly as she wedged it securely between the frame and the window. The outside air seemed to suck the smoke out of the kitchen.

She rushed for the door and stepped outside for fresh air. Just as she took in a deep breath, the door locked behind her.

"Oh, great! Now what?"

She sat on the step and put her face in her hands. She pulled the white piece of her mostly strawberry blond hair to twirl like she always did when she was thinking. It reeked of the charred cheese soup.

His words played back to her. "If you don't have a key, you aren't getting back inside."

No house key, no car key, no cell phone, no brain! What a mess I have gotten myself into this time.

The noise from the large oak tree seemed to be laughing at her as the wind blew down dried leaves like rotten tomatoes for a bad performance.

Jay always shows up at unexpected times. Why not now?

Her sweater was draped on the chair just on the other side of the door. How nice it would feel draped over her shoulders. How she wished for it now. Not only would it block some of the chill in the air, but also the keys were in the pocket.

Wasn't this just like life? You try to get out of one situation only to find yourself in a worse one. I jumped out of the smoky house and into the cold.

Prism's barking could be heard inside the locked house.

Open the bedroom door, girl and then open this one.

"Come, Prism! Good, girl!" Laven yelled trying to encourage her to use her door opening skills.

"Prism!"

Laven heard a clanging sound. Had Prism gotten herself out of the bedroom?

"Prism, come girl!"

The leaves rustled, but beyond she heard a muffled crackling sound like that caused by the movement of dry leaves.

Prism continued to bark, but Laven heard a definite crunching sound as though someone was running on dry leaves.

She walked to the side of the house where the noise might have come from. There was no one in sight. She saw no reason for the noise. The tall lilac bushes moved, but it was likely due to a wind current. She looked up at the window holding the box of chocolates and just below it was a wooden planter that she hadn't noticed before.

"You just might be my lucky break!"

It is when you talk to a wooden box that you know you are desperate. Now how do I do this?

Laven was known for being klutzy. She was always the last to be picked for team sports. She stood wondering how to navigate herself into the house by way of the planter.

Steadying herself by placing her hand on the side of

the house, she stepped up on the wooden box. It needed to be about a foot higher for convenience. She hoisted herself up not twice but three times before finally managing to get her arms hooked over the window frame. She made writhing movements until she was nearly to her waist inside the window.

Now what to do?

She was squeezed next to the chocolate box. If she pushed it out, the window would come crashing down on her. There was no room to bring a leg up. Her hourglass figure was not a positive attribute at this moment. She was stuck.

Heads I'm in. Tails I'm out. I am neither in nor out. I lose.

She could hear a ruckus from upstairs and then a white mass of curls came bounding into the kitchen.

Prism shared some dog breath along with a literal tongue-lashing and then began to growl.

Her ears moved back and then she barked viciously and headed for the back door.

Laven pulled and twisted to get herself through the window. And then she heard it, a door slammed shut.

"Prism!"

Prism continued to bark, but came running to Laven.

"Was that you? Did you open the back door? If so, I wish you would have done it sooner, before I got myself in this predicament."

Laven kicked her feet like paddling air would help her through the window. It didn't. Should she just drop?

No, I don't want this lucky break to break my leg. The last thing I want is a trip back to the hospital.

Nothing was within reach for leverage. She was just as much in as she was out.

She began a tumultuous wiggling motion as much out of anger as of despair. Then she heard a loud bang and screeching brakes.

She didn't know whether to be relieved or not. This was truly an awkward position.

When Jay walked up to her, she was glad that embarrassment only showed on the heads portion of her.

"What have we here? Are you going in or coming out?"

"Neither at the moment."

"What tells me that you forgot your key?"

"Are you just going to stand down there or give me a hand? And I don't mean applause either."

"Balance is concerned about horizontal motion. You have accomplished that. You have the force concentrated on your waist."

"Could you please save the physic's lesson for when we are both in a vertical. standing position?"

"How about you slide your feet down and I will lift you up. That would be the most appropriate place for me to hold you."

"Okay." Laven blushed as she lowered her feet down and into his hands. She then felt herself being raised up and through the window. Her fingers touched the floor and she hand -walked until all of her was inside the kitchen.

~

They sat on each end of the sofa. Laven sat sideways

with her feet on the cushion to ensure distance was kept. Although the stench of burnt soup in her hair might help steer him clear of her.

"Oh, you have to see what I found today!" Prism followed her closely into the kitchen.

Jay laughed hearing Laven singing at her with each step. "I don't like you. I don't like you!"

He joined them in the kitchen.

"What is that?" He asked looking at the charred pan.

Laven answered a little embarrassed. "It's my incinerated cheese soup that I wanted to surprise you with." She took the blackened pan and dropped it into the empty garbage receptacle.

"I propped the window open with this to let the smoke out." She removed the box of candy from the window and it slammed shut with a clicking of the lock. The lid of the box was loose so she maneuvered it carefully to keep the chocolates from falling out.

"Lula gave me these. Care for one?"

"No thanks."

Laven placed the box back in the cabinet with the glass door and looked down at the counter.

"It's gone! Jay, it was right here inside a scrapbook. They are both gone!"

"Maybe you placed them somewhere else and forgot. I do that some times."

"No! They were here when the smoke was in the kitchen and now they are gone! Someone took them! Someone got in the house and stole them

Laven was visibly shaken so Jay convinced her to go back in the living room to sit down.

"What was it?"

"It was the magnifying glass. The one my mother spoke of with her last breath. There was something about it she wanted me to know and now I never will."

"Tell me what you remember about it?"

"It was a large magnifying glass, very ornate. It was an antique. The word, 'Sterling' was inscribed on it, but it didn't appear to be silver."

Laven put her head in her hands.

"Now I will never know why she wanted me to see it."

"I will check the pawn shops to see if someone tries to sell it. Do you really think that someone was in the house?"

"I know the book and magnifying glass didn't just walk away or blow out of the window with the smoke.

I heard the back door slam shut when I was stuck in the window. Someone must have already been in the house. I was on the front porch for quite awhile. They could have come through the window."

There was a noise in the kitchen, but it would have to wait. She was too upset to care at the moment. She sat in a disappointed suspension, like a living statue.

Jay walked around to see if he could find the magnifying glass or any indication that someone uninvited had entered.

Laven finally looked around. The white furry nuisance wasn't irritating her.

"Prism, come!" The dog didn't obey. After repeating her name several times, Laven finally went into the kitchen.

Chapter 11

~~~

"JAY!" LAVEN SCREAMED.

Jay ran to the kitchen and found Laven over Prism's outstretched body.

"What happened?"

"She jumped up and got into the chocolates!"

"We have to get her to the vet," Jay said as he lifted the huge white limp bulk. Laven looked at the chocolates on the floor and the few remaining in the box.

Laven sat in the back seat with her as they rushed to

the animal hospital. "Don't die, girl. Don't die."

The dog was immediately taken to the back of the clinic while Laven and Jay sat in the waiting room and did exactly what the room was designed for.

They sat silently for what seemed hours when a Veterinarian Technician came into the room.

"The Dr. wants to keep her under observation so you can come back in a couple of hours if you would like."

"Is she going to be alright?"

"The doctor will discuss her condition when you return."

"Okay, thanks."

"Shall we go to the Sip and Chew for a quick bite to eat?" Jay suggested.

"Just as well."

He grinned at Laven and started to speak but stopped himself.

"What?" Laven urged him to continue.

"Later, now is not the time."

He is making a habit of almost telling me something. Something that time and circumstances seem to matter.

"Shouldn't we turn here?"

"Hey, you are pretty good." He responded with a grin.

"At what, being a back seat driver? That's about all I'm good at."

"We'll take a short cut."

"Aren't all routes short in this little town?"

"Well, we will take an alternate route. Quit putting yourself down."

"I should have been watching Prism more closely."

"I thought you didn't like her."

"I don't like her, but that doesn't mean I want her dead."

They pulled up to the Diner. Jay walked around the car to open the door for her. He pulled at the handle, but nothing happened.

"Could you jiggle the door handle?"

Laven followed the instructions. Jay hit the side of the door and pulled the handle again and it finally opened.

"Sorry about that. The mechanism must have jammed."

"I am becoming adapted to doors locking behind me."

"Look, our table is available," Jay announced as he pointed through the window.

"Our table?"

"Yeah, the one we sat at the last time we were here," he said as he led Laven inside the restaurant. Just inside the door something made him stop and change his mind.

"Let's not eat here tonight. I know another place."

Laven was curious as to why the change of mind, but asked no questions.

"I am more in the mood for Mexican food.

Remember those great chimichangas? Let's do those instead."

"Sounds good to me." Laven wondered if that was the real reason he left the Sip and Chew.

Festive Spanish music could be heard from the parking lot. She glanced around the restaurant. It was dark with a glow of candles in red glass globes. The tables had red and white checked tablecloths like the kind you might use at a picnic.

"What the ambiance lacks the food more than adjusts for."

The waitress brought them a basket of chips and salsa.

"My turn to buy tonight. After all, I more than scorched our soup."

He spoke as though she had said nothing. "It's all about the sauce. They make it right here. Everything is made with fresh ingredients, and no lard."

A distinguished looking man approached their table and said with a slight Spanish accent. "Well, it's good to see you, my friend. Your dinner is on me. I owe you one."

"No, No."

"I insist. And who is your beautiful companion?"

"This is Laven. Laven, this is mi amigo, Ricardo. " Jay smiled.

"I see no ring upon her finger. Someone who brings a smile so big to your face, you must not let get away." He let out a contagious laugh that blanketed the embarrassment of the moment. The man kept laughing as he left.

"Everywhere you go you score a deal!" Laven spoke quickly to change the subject. "Okay, the next one is on me."

He is staring at me.

"Is it your intention to make me feel uncomfortable at every restaurant ?"

"No. It's just that at a restaurant is the only time I get to look into your eyes."

"I can't eat when you are staring at me."

"Did I tell you that you have beautiful eyes? They

have flecks of gold."

"What are you a gold digger?" Laven wished that she could retract her words as soon as she had spoken them. That was the stupidest thing she could have said.

"I have been accused of a lot of things but not that. So no, are you?"

"No, and I am not a car thief either."

Laven, keep your mouth shut! Your lack of social skills is becoming apparent.

She dunked a chip into the salsa. "This is very good."

She spoke sparingly and listened as Jay described the difference between corn chips and tortilla chips. He prefers tortilla chips, which have been subjected to a process that has umpteen letters in the name and results in a milder flavor and less salt than corn chips.

I had hoped that his font could help me learn the significance of the magnifying glass. Now I will never know what she was trying to tell me through it. Does everything connected to my mother have to be mysterious or absent of any importance just as she was absent from my life?

"Would you like to try some fried ice cream?"

"No, thank you. That was really good. Please thank Ricardo for me."

"Oh, I'm sure you will see him again," he said as he walked her to the car.

The door didn't open on the first try, but a jolt with his open palm seemed to do the job.

"You direct me back to the animal clinic."

"Not fair, you used a short cut that I am not familiar with and besides it is getting dark. I hope she is okay."

The doctor met them in the waiting room.

"Your dog was poisoned, but not by chocolate. It would take over sixty pounds of chocolate to poison a dog her size. You need to check for other sources of poison in your home. Here are your instructions for her care."

Laven paid the bill and Jay helped Prism back to the car.

Poison?

Had Lula given her chocolates laced with poison? But why would she? Had someone tampered with them? No, they were wrapped in cellophane. But wait, the cellophane wasn't on the box when she removed it from the window.

The poison wasn't meant for Prism.

Chapter 12

~~~

LAVEN HAD CHECKED THE chocolates as soon as they returned from the animal hospital. She examined closely the ones with no bite marks and found a small needle hole in each. There was no cellophane to be found.

The law enforcement team listened to her story and took notes but since the victim wasn't a human being, they didn't seem to place as much importance on the event as she had hoped.

They probably think I staged trying to murder the dog to bring attention to myself to try to divert their focus away from the stolen car.

It had been quiet around the house while Prism

recuperated. She enjoyed an occasional fast food cheeseburger and now she was beginning to get back to her old bouncy self. She didn't seem to have an allergic reaction to the junk food.

Laven considered it as an alternative to the expensive natural blend, but decided she had best keep her healthy if she wanted to find her a good home.

Her bark let Laven know that someone was coming to the door. It allowed time to descend the stairs before the knock sounded. She used even more caution than usual after the poisoning incident. How much longer would her threatener give her to leave?

The peek hole revealed a uniformed deliveryman with a letter. Laven slowly opened the door.

"Miss Hoddy?"

"Yes."

"I have a certified letter for you. Please sign here."

She signed on the board a scribble that looked

nothing like her signature. The man thanked her and hurried to his van.

There was no return address and she hadn't requested a receipt.

She carefully opened the envelope and was shocked at what it held. She looked at the title of Lula's Mercedes Benz. She had signed the car over to Laven. There was a small handwritten note which read

The car is yours, dear.

Drive it out of Rising Springs as soon as possible.

Ship the bed!

It is not safe for you there.

Sincerely, Lula

There was no return address. There was no one to discuss what had just happened.

Was it for real? Her first thought was that if Lula was going to give her a car, then she probably didn't try to poison her. The title looked authentic. She had no way of contacting Lula to thank her or to ask about the danger here.

It seemed like one event loaded on top of another before she had time to process the first. It would be good to leave this place. Lula didn't have to tell her to leave. It was in her plan to do so.

Like the bed and dog, she had no use for a flashy sports car. Her nice economy car at home was perfect for staying under the radar both figurative and literally.

It was good on gas and easy to maneuver in traffic.

She would have Jay help her sell the black shiny convertible. Then an idea hit her.

"Yes! That will be perfect! I will give him the car. It will more than pay him back for all that he has done for me.

And it is definitely something he desperately needs!"

Brain, I like the way you are working! I am not one of those people who would never pay him back. The only rush he will get from this deal is the one from owning such a fine-looking vehicle.

Laven felt good to be back in power.

Music sounded on her phone indicating a text message was sent to her.

Perfect timing!

"Are you busy?" He asked electronically.

"I'm strenuously encountering a laborious effort." She teased.

"May I offer my assistance?"

"That would only escalate my challenge."

"Try me. I'll help you solve your dilemma. Allow me to suspend your predicament."

I am pushing to extend my gray matter in an attempt to develop a clever presentation for your present."

"A lagniappe for me?"

"No, but I doubt that you will have an objection to this object."

"Ha! A lagniappe is a complicated way to say gift. I am on my way."

And here I thought he was dreaming of a pasta dish of some kind.

~

Laven heard Prism's warning bark from upstairs. She didn't need it to know that Jay would soon knock on the door. The shrill screech of the worn brakes told the story loudly.

She grabbed her purse and opened the house door before he could convince the car door to open.

Laven smiled a hello at him.

"The other one now, huh?"

"Yeah, this is the first time this one has stuck. I need to add both doors to my fix-it list."

The fix-it list for this rattletrap could run the length of the continental divide. He will be happy to know that he can pitch the list along with this mess of metal when I give him his gift. He's right. It's a great feeling to give someone something that they can't repay.

She gave herself a mental pat on the back for coming up with the idea. It was a good one.

"Let's take a ….

"You read my mind! I have something to show you." He interrupted not even mentioning his gift.

"Mercedes?" Remembering the dark haired girl, she quickly rephrased. "Do you want to take the convertible?"

"No, I just filled ole Patch's tank."

That was a waste of money!

Jay attempted to open the passenger door for Laven, but it wasn't until he gave it an open palm punch that he succeeded.

She gave herself another pat on the back in her mind for coming up with this idea. If ever there was a need for an improvement, she was sitting in it.

The ride down Chequered Lane may as well been on horseback Laven thought, bracing herself through the bumpy ride. Once they turned the corner at the intersection, it seemed to smoothen and give her back a rest.

"You turned the wrong way."

"Some backseat driver you are." Jay smiled and Laven felt the heat it sent. "You need to ascertain the destination before you determine we are headed in the wrong direction.""I'll jot that down for next time," she said as the road darkened. "May I inquire where you have determined our destination will be?"

She felt a bit nervous going out of town. Her concern was not so much for being alone with Jay, but being in Patch on a deserted piece of highway.

"I am going to show you a body."

Perhaps my concern should shift.

"A body like in dead?"

"A body like in a body of water."

Whew!

"And if my timing isn't off, you will see suspended in the sky, a moon you will desire to capture on stretched canvas. The lake is a horizontal mirror to reflect its magnificence."

The blue sky slid behind the horizon and in its place a blanket of dark indigo arose. Then just as promised, an enormous orange sphere made its appearance over the sparkling, dark water of the lake.

The two sat in agreed awe of the picture before them. There were no words that could adequately describe the scene. So, appropriately, no words were spoken.

Laven wanted it never to end, but clouds began to float over the yellowing globe veiling it from their view. It soon appeared to diminish into an ordinary, every night moon.

She began to wonder if this celestial show would devalue her gift.

"That was amazing," she sighed.

"It's never wasted time to spend it reveling over God's handiwork."

"You won't find this a waste of time either. It's time for your pasta dish word, AKA your gift." She opened her purse and pulled out the key to the Mercedes. She flicked it open and the key swung out of the casing.

"Whoa! That looked like a miniature switchblade at first."

"Here," she said as she handed him the key.

"What's this?"

"You are now the owner of a black SLK Mercedes."

Jay laughed. "Our girl, Lula might have an objection to that notion."

"She gave it to me. The title is in my name. I am re-gifting and signing it over to you."

Jay stared at Laven. It was difficult to read his expression in the dark.

"I can't accept this."

"Why, it's not the car for one who wishes to remain invisible."

"It's most generous and thoughtful of you, but it's a gift I can't receive."

"But, why? Nothing is expected of you. There are no strings."

"Laven, this is unbelievable that you would try to gift me with a car, but I really don't need it. If you truly don't want it, you could donate it to the poor."

That's what I am trying to do, silly!

"Jay, put your pride aside. You need it!"

"I really don't."

"If it's the size, you could either sell it or trade it for a larger vehicle."

He tried to touch her, but Laven pulled away.

"This is really touching, Laven."

You can say it, but just don't try doing it.

Jay placed the key back into Laven's hand.

"We'll discuss this later," he said, as he tried to start the engine, and tried...and tried.

Laven turned her head to the window to hide the smirk on her face.

He doesn't need a car. Yeah, right.

Jay shook the door handle until it opened, stepped out and lifted the hood.

This guy is delusional not to know he desperately

needs a car.

Whatever he did seemed a temporary fix on permanent problem on four wheels.

Jay turned on the one-station radio, which broke the silence on the trip back.

At least one gift was appreciated. Laven pushed back mounting disappointment of her great idea not being accepted.

The clouds were blocking the stars, but it was the laced canopy of tree branches that made it officially dark.

"Look!" Laven called out without warning. But no sooner than the word was spoken was it no longer needed. The light was no longer showing in the nearest house on Chequered Lane.

"What?"

"Nothing." Laven decided not to mention what she had seen because, like the blue painted warning, the light vanished before other eyes could witness it.

A CLOSER LOOK

PAMELA FERNANDEZ

Chapter 13

~~~

LAVEN HOPED TO NEVER forget the sight of the gigantic orange ball suspended over the lake. She remembered free falling down to earth from two miles high. There is no end to the sky and no end to its wonders. It goes all the way to where God is. He is here and there and everywhere as is the sky.

Somewhere up there, clouds were colliding. Their rumble could be heard rolling up above. Dark clouds threatened, but no water fell.

Prism barked ferociously making it impossible to enjoy God's trombones.

"That's not a knocking at the door. It's a knocking in the sky. Sit still and stay clean. I would like to list you online but I don't have time. I wonder what the shipping would be on a pet the size of a horse?"

Prism was persistent. She hadn't been a false alarm yet. Each time she sent her barking advisory, someone had come to the door.

Just to make sure, she followed the back-to-good health, unwanted, inheritance down the stairs. The peek hole revealed nothing.

"There is a first time for everything. You are wrong. No one is there."

Prism barked as if in an argumentative manner.

"Okay. Look!"

Laven opened the door and it was she who looked. A rectangular, leather covered package laid on the step. It was tied with a darker leather strap.

She stepped out and looked in both directions before picking it up.

There was not a soul in sight. Looking down at the hide-covered package, she scolded herself silently for touching the undetermined object with exposed fingerprints.

Prism sniffed at it excitedly. "No nose prints!"

She carried it into the kitchen and placed it on the counter while she pulled on the yellow gloves she found under the sink.

She fumbled at the knot in the leather cord but found it impossible to untie using rubber fingers, which extended an inch and a half beyond her own.

Frustrated, she pulled out the kitchen sheers and cut the cord. She peeled the hide back carefully not knowing what it contained. There inside, was a paperback book with what once held blank pages.

They were no longer blank, but now contained letters of all shapes and sizes taped to every page. Each page read, "Leave," in an assortment of fonts and colors.

She awkwardly thumbed through the book. Each page held the same letters, each page looked different, but the warning was the same. Laven stopped where the book ended on the back paper cover.

This page was unlike the others.

All the previous pages presented a warning; this

page presented an ultimatum, the results of not heading the warning. The paper book had an

unhappy ending.

The letters seemed to be written in red paint, but the appearance was more like blood. Drips of dried, red, scrawled letters seemed to scream, "Or Die!"

Laven took a step back. Should she call Jay? Was he the one who created this stuck- together threat? Had he kept the magazines instead of throwing them away? Had he carefully cut each letter and joined them together to send me a message.

But why would he show me so much attention if he wanted me to die?

She pulled off the rubber gloves, reached for her phone and dialed 911.

~

The uniformed officers who had become frequent visitors followed Laven into the kitchen. She showed them the bound-together pages of threats. They placed the paperback warning into a plastic bag with protected hands.

The policeman wrote as Laven gave her account of how the threatening paper book made its way to the kitchen counter.

"I only touched the leather with bare prints." Laven announced proudly.

But instead of a, 'job well done look,' the policeman frowned her way.

Prism barked lightly and whipped around her tail like a windmill in a storm. Seconds later, Jay knocked at the door.

Does he have you fooled too or are you in cahoots with him. Every time an incident occurs, Jay happens.

"What's going on?!"

"Someone wrote, published, and delivered a paperback to me. There was no title, but had there been, it should have read, "Leave.""

"May I see it?"

The police already have it packaged for evidence or inspection or whatever they do with the things they take from here.

All I know is that I've already read it and I didn't like the ending."

~

There was a promise from the men in blue to increase surveillance and keep a presence in the area.

Jay had offered to be with her today, but Laven had insisted on being alone.

She had to sort out the all the things churning in her mind. Either Jay was exceptionally good at acting or her armor had been so badly damaged by his kindness that she was blinded. His actions along with his words indicated he wanted her to stay. Why would he then try to scare her into leaving?

The clouds formed together and collectively spilled out rain. Thunder belted out in 'surround sound'. Had any tears remained, she might have used them now. Instead, she let the sky do it for her.

Laven sat on her inherited bed and wrapped herself in her own arms. The room darkened and Prism jumped up with her. The big, bad-barking watchdog now needed protection.

Laven wondered if she needed protection.

Her thoughts went to Jay. She struggled to decide if she really knew him.

If his pride ran so deep as to prefer to drive that unreliable heap, then so be it.

The rhythm of the rain relaxed her and the next thing she knew, she was waking up in a cuddled position with a large mass of white fur. Prism began to sound her visitor warning bark, which had proven to be correct one hundred per cent of the time.

 "I don't like you!"

Prism continued to bark and Laven heard the forewarned knock on the door. The large animal led her down the stairs.

She was right again. The peek hole revealed a man in a uniform.

Now what?

Laven opened the door cautiously, holding Prism back.

"Hello, I have an order here to install security cameras."

"I didn't order any cameras."

"Yes, but the owner of the property decided to have them installed after some reported potential criminal activity. Please sign here."

The man handed her a covered clipboard containing an invoice. She pulled it inside to avoid getting it wet.

She read down to the bottom of the form looking to

see the name of the new owner. Apparently the property had been turned over for a judge to handle. Laven signed her name.

"The rain has let up. It should only take me a couple of hours to complete unless the rain picks up again.

"Do I need to be here?"

"Not initially. I will install the cameras around the perimeter of the house first."

"Do I have time to run into town for some groceries?" Laven asked, feeling confident that a judge knew about the threat.

"That will be fine."

Laven took Prism back upstairs against the dog's consent.

"I am going to town to get some groceries. You are not!"

She left the sad eyes of the large animal in the bedroom, grabbed her things, and left the security man installing cameras which would capture all activity including her own.

The rain had reduced to a light sprinkle. The air smelled newly laundered. As she breathed in the fresh air, she remembered that everything wasn't new here.

There were unresolved problems that stained her life.

The area was becoming familiar. Laven could find her way around town. She couldn't decide if that was a good thing or a bad thing. Time was running out. There were only days left until her leave would end and she would be expected back in her stark grey cubicle. At least things made sense there.

She remembered when she had first requested time off. It was suppose to be for time spent with the mother she had never known. Instead, it had been used on the importance of an antique magnifying glass and keeping herself out of jail.

As she searched for the windshield wipers to clear the blurred visibility, a thought struck her.

I can use bereavement leave. This is the only time I can use it on my solitary relative.

With the approved time off, I won't have to divulge information on the ever-growing police investigation encircling me.

And then there was the dilemma with Jay.

He was the closest thing she had ever had to a friend and she was bound and determined that he wouldn't get close to being anything more. She thought of his irresistible smile and the knack he had for finding great deals, on everything, that is, except a vehicle.

Calling that car a lemon would be a verbal assault on the yellow fruit. For some reason he liked it. He liked it so much that he turned down this car to continue adding to the fix-it list. His pride cost

When she closed the door of the shiny, black sports car, she noted the limited space in the trunk for groceries.

She would have to be selective even on the few items needed for the limited days that remained.

Size was as important if not more important than price, she decided as she compared both before placing an item in the shopping cart.

She was reading the ingredients on the package to ensure the packaging didn't contain more nutrients than the product when someone with a face that looked familiar interrupted her.

She looked back at the woman who seemed to be challenging her to a stare down.

"I have been racking my brain trying to place you and it finally hit me!"

"Have we met?" Laven asked with a polite smile.

"Not exactly, but I saw you in our old car with Mr. Well."

Laven finally remembered where she had seen the woman and her smile faded from her face. She was with the rude family who had pulled up beside Jay to mock him for driving such a junky car. She had been seated in the passenger seat motioning for him to roll down his window so he could better hear their insults.

Wait, did she say that junky car once belonged to

them?

"Meeting him was like winning the jack pot for us. He is the nicest, most generous guy ever! We were stranded beside the road.

The kids were hungry and crying and the car wouldn't start. This has been a really rough year for us until he came along.

When he pulled over we thought he was going to jump the battery for us but, instead, he jumped in the front seat and told us to take his card and his car!

The next day he made arrangements for us to trade

vehicles! We are still in disbelief. Please tell Mr. Well thank you again for us. We can't thank him enough for what he did."

"Mr. Well? You must be...

"Oh, I've got to run. Nice talking to you. Bye.

Laven followed the lady with her eyes as she literally ran down the aisle. She arrived at the end of the shelf just in time to break the fall of the toddler who had unsuccessfully made the attempt to become part of the display rack.

Mr. Well? Had she been talking about Jay? Pressure squeezed across her chest.

I have foolishly invested trust in him. Was Mercedes' warning legitimate when she cautioned that he wasn't who he claimed to be?

All the questions about him congregated in her brain forming one big suspicion.

He had been there for the car wreck. He arrived a little too conveniently when the rock smashed through the window.

When he was looking around the house, he might have had time to inject the chocolates with poison.

When he hauled the magazines out of the house, did he place them into the trunk of his garbage can car instead of the trash bin?

Did he wear the mask of a clandestine villain to make a grand entrance as a hero?

But, why? I have nothing. I am nothing. I am

certainly not worth the effort.

She was in total confusion when she paid for her groceries and made her way to the parking lot. There, several rows over, the lady wrestled her unruly toddler into a beautiful new car.

She wanted more than ever to leave this state along with this state of confusion,

Should she confront Jay or whatever his real name is or let him keep playing his game of deception to see where it leads?

Her chest tightened to a level of pain realized that, though she had tried to resist, she had allowed herself to trust him. He had turned that trust into a dagger and pierced her heart. She had tasted the food of a fool.

Chapter 14

~~~

LAVEN STOOD AT THE DOOR staring into Jay's eyes. The mirror to his soul was deceptive because his gaze seemed clear and decent.

"Are you going to ask me in?"

"I was taught by the nuns not to talk to strangers."

"Laven, you look hurt. What is the matter?"

She opened the door for him to enter.

"Are you going to tell me what's wrong?" Jay's eyes were now filled with concern.

I'm pushing. I'm pushing, but he keeps getting

closer. My barriers are weakening. I must be strong and resist the urge to give him one more inch of trust. I've let this go too far. I am going to get hurt and it will be a result of my own stupidity, my own weakness. I won't stand with my hand on the window and hope anymore. The pain will be less if I end this before he does. He will, so I must. If I don't protect me, no one will. I not only know lonely, I am lonely. There is safety and comfort in accepting who I am.

"You have been kind to me and shown me some wonderful experiences, but it's time to break free from whatever we have here."

"Laven, I don't want to diminish in anyway the pain you have gone through. The story of your childhood is heartbreaking. But you haven't dealt with it and now it is dealing with you.

You've allowed yourself to be kept captive there and the child of the past keeps hurting you over and over."

"You live your life and I'll live mine."

"You aren't living your life, Laven. You are bound in the chains of the past. Instead of breaking free from what you have, you need to break free from your childhood."

"It's so easy for you to say."

"As much as you are allowing the pain of yesterday to hurt you, it's actually the easy way out. You need to take action. Lean into God and He will lean into you and break those chains of the past that keep you weighted down."

"You don't understand."

"You aren't the only one who has experienced pain. We all have challenges in this life. Believe it or not some have experienced so much more than you. God's mercy gives us hope. Let that dangling H in your name be for Hope. Let God fill you with his love and mercy."

"Hopeless would be more fitting."

"In some sick way, you are enjoying your pain. Learn to trust, Laven."

"That's rich coming from the lips of a liar."

Jay stared at Laven with confusion in his eyes.

"As it turns out, Jay Shane doesn't exist. Does he,

Mr. Well?"

"I didn't lie, Laven. Everything I have ever told you has been the truth."

"You said your name was Jay Shane."

"Some people do call me Jay. You know Jay use to be slang used to describe a foolish person, hence the expression jaywalker. Boy, have I been foolish! I shouldn't have left you hanging with the unfinished truth, even though J is my first initial and Shane is my middle name.

I wanted so many times to tell you my full name, but there were either interruptions or the timing wasn't right."

"You led me to believe you were broke with the car you drove."

"You surmised that on your own. I told you I traded for it."

"Yeah, a brand new car that neither stalled nor backfired."

"Like I can not personally understand what you have been through, neither can you relate to the way I have been hurt. I don't want someone to love me for my money or car. I want to be loved for whom I am inside. If everything I have leaves, I'll be just me."

Laven rummaged through past conversations trying to pull up other lies.

"You told me that you worked at the Well Wishes restaurant as a dish washer."

"That's not a lie. I do work there when they are shorthanded. I am the owner."

Laven swallowed hard as it came together in her mind. Well Wishes-His name was in the name.

"So how rich are you?"

"I'm not rich. Everything that God has given me is His. When a prospective girlfriend finds that I tithe to myself, I'm dropped like a bad habit."

"Tithe to yourself?"

"Yeah, ninety percent is God's and I live on the remaining tenth portion of earnings. It's crazy to some, but I am blessed beyond measure."

"You've made a fool of me. I would have respected

you had you been honest with me, but you entertained me with half-truths. You've gone to extreme lengths," Then remembering the skydive, she continued, "And extreme heights to gain my trust and it was all a test."

"I feel as though you've tested me too, Laven."

"And how is that?"

"To see if you could trust me. I tried to prove that you could."

"Well, you failed the test! Look, I just addressed you with your real name."

"Maybe I did fail, Laven, but God won't fail you. Trust Him to make all things perfect. He will turn all those tragic things that happened to you into good for your life."

"I asked this question before, but I will give it another shot and hope for the truth this time. What is your name?"

"My name is Justice Well."

"Okay, goodbye, Justice."

What kind of name is Justice? Did his mom think she

was giving birth to a future judge or something?

All at once her memory seemed to close in on the security camera invoice. Justice Well, who as it turns out, was no judge, ordered it. Jay was the owner of her Mother's house.

It was difficult for Laven to speak. "My mother left her house to you!"

She didn't know which to assign the pain to, Jay or her mother.

Jay tried to speak.

"You knew all the time and didn't tell me!" Her words were marbled with hurt and anger.

"Laven, I never met your mother. She didn't leave the house to me. She left it to one of my charitable foundations. The one I am probably the most passionate about. Women are denigrated and even used as a lucrative commodity by some very evil people. I had no knowledge of the transaction until I was with you at the reading of the will.

I was shocked to learn she assigned the property for that purpose. I was trying to start a home for girls rescued from human trafficking and the sex trade.

Your mother must have heard about it and thought it was a worthy cause."

"You knew all this time and didn't tell me."

"I have spoken to my attorneys to see how I can purchase the property from the foundation and give it to you." I was waiting to see if you wanted it. I thought it might have a negative feel over it since your mother hadn't left it to you in the first place."

"Save your time. I don't want it."

"I didn't think so, but if you find a place you do like, I will buy it for you in exchange."

"Save your tithe. I don't want it. I don't need your charity."

The exchange of words gnawed at her stomach causing her to feel nauseous.

"Laven, you don't know how touched I am that you offered to give me Lula's car. That showed me that you cared."

"It shouldn't have. The car cost me nothing and meant nothing to me and I owed you. It was nothing more than paying a debt

"But, Laven..

She could tell her words had wounded him. Now one final punch for the knock out blow and this will all be over. She just hadn't anticipated how much it hurts to hurt others.

"You need to leave now."

"Something supernatural is going to happen in your heart and God's love is going to grow. You will experience His unlimited love."

"And how do you know that? Is it from your font of useless information?!"

"No, it's from my prayer closet."

"It's not for me."

"It's not all about you, Laven. You need to get over yourself. It's arrogant of you to think you can control your life better than the one who created you."

"I am a product of life's hard knocks that were allowed to happen to me."

"Don't wait until you are truly knocked down before you reach for God."

"Not only do I not want to hear your lies, I don't want to see you anymore."

"I am not lying, Laven. I bought these tickets for a day cruise on the lake. If you change your mind about seeing me, I'll be there."

Laven kept her arms tightly folded so Jay tossed the ticket on the sofa and walked out of her life.

Just as well.

The words echoed in her ear. Laven now understood the smile he displayed every time she uttered that expression. She was phonetically pronouncing his true name each time she said it.

I'll never again use that phrase.

Chapter 15

~~~

"YOU ARE A MONSTROUS nightmare!"

The two stared at each other.

"If I could locate Lula, she would get you back along with her car. I don't like you.

You have complicated my life."

Prism panted happily.

"At least you are healthy again.

This is the perfect time to place an advertisement in the paper for you. It'll say 'free dog.' She remembered that people will usually take better care of the pet if they have invested in.

"It'll say $100, no $50, and I will go down quickly to $0 without much of a negotiation."

"You are going to the groomer," she informed Prism as they climbed the stairs. "No cutesy French cuts for you, I'll have you shaved so that I don't have to bother brushing you."

"There's something else that needs to be done and I just as well...oops." She said his name accidentally as she was speaking aloud to herself.

He had told her that it takes 56 days to break a habit. She wondered how long it would take for her to get him out of her mind.

She pulled the folder that was given to her by Larson E. Cruque containing instructions for her mother's ashes.

She jotted down the address, closed Prism in the bedroom, and headed for the garage.

As she drove down Checquered Lane, she thought she saw movement at the neighboring house, but saw nothing on the second glance.

The GPS directed her to the building that kept her mother's remains.

She was surprised after providing her signature to receive a box, which appeared to be made of onyx.

She had expected an urn of some kind. There was a clasp but no keyhole. A picture of a woman holding a child's hand was carved on the top. It didn't seem to be an appropriate representation for ashes to be held in, but then she had not intended for her ashes to remain in the box.

Since the portion of her mother that matters wasn't actually present, she placed the green stone box in the trunk and drove to the address to place the ad in the newspaper.

That was easy enough. Now if someone will want the dreadful beast, we will all be happy.

Earlier, she had spotted an interesting shop and decided to stop and see if she could find a jacket. She had only brought the sweater and there was nothing to wear while it was being cleaned.

She tried on several different light coats, but it was

the white one that brought complimentary remarks from the sales attendant. "That looks beautiful on you!"

Laven knew that the girl was only trying to make a commission on her purchase.

Besides, there was no reason to try to look beautiful.

White wasn't the most practical color, but she decided to buy it anyway. She blamed it on comfort.

On the way back to the house, Laven replayed the exchange she had with Jay over in her mind as many times as he had listened to the songs on his radio station.

She wondered if she could have said goodbye in a more charitable way. He had really done nothing to her. She had done it to herself by lowering her guard. The goodbye was necessary, but the knock out punch was not.

When she closed the self-locking door, she decided that she didn't like herself very much.

Prism came bounding down the stairs to meet her.

"Hey, how did you get out? I'd better see if the door is still standing."

The door was standing, but Prism had carved a patch in the wall with her claws. There were also bite marks on the floorboard. "You are wrecking Mr. Well's house!

I hope we can find a new home for you soon."

She climbed onto her bequeathed brass bed. Being mean felt miserable to Laven. She didn't wear it well. It in no way fit her.

She used to wonder how the kids at the orphanage and foster care could be so hurtful. Now she was very close to being one of them herself.

I don't want to let my defenses down and care about Jay or Justice or whatever his name is but I need to apologize for treating him so badly. After all he has been supportive.

She picked up her phone and sent him a text message.

"I need to talk."

Laven was beginning to think he wasn't going to respond, but finally a message popped up on her phone.

"1:00 p.m." is all the reply said.

This time she intentionally spent extra time in front of the mirror. Someone who acted so ugly should look extra pretty when trying to make it right. She was dabbing on some perfume when Prism began her pre-knock warning.

Laven hurried down the stairs when the knock sounded at exactly 1:00 p.m.

He's never late.

Not even bothering with the peek hole, she swung the door open.

Laven's eyes opened wide as she stood stunned as the handsome man spoke.

"Hello, I'm Trey Lucas, a friend of Well's. He asked me to stop by and see you. He said that you needed to talk."

Laven was speechless. She had been thrown away again, given to someone else to deal with. She had been kicked to the side like a piece of garbage.

"There was just a communication glitch. I said some things to him that I now regret and I just wanted to apologize."

He mentioned that you had some things in your past that continue to haunt you. Perhaps it would help to talk and get to the genesis of your problems."

"No, that won't be necessary, but thanks anyway."

"Are you sure? I believe I can at least give you some tools to help you work through your issues."

"I'm sure."

Jay had given her a counter punch after the match was over. I guess this was his way of saying whatever they had, really was over.

"Let me leave you my card. Please give me a call if you change your mind. I'd love to try to work with you."

Laven politely accepted the business card. It wasn't

this nice looking guy's fault that he had been used as a weapon against her.

"By the way, you have beautiful eyes. They hold golden flecks."

"Thanks, that's been mentioned to me before."

She wondered if she should wear dark glasses as she closed the door to end the conversation.

She closed the door and looked down at the card the handsome visitor had given her. Her throat choked as she read, Dr. Trey Lucas, psychologist.

He thinks I'm mentally unstable! Is it possible for empty to grow emptier?

It was time to tie up the remaining loose ends and pack her self out of here.

She would arrange for the brass bed to be shipped. Hopefully, she would receive a response on Prism in the next 24 hours.

For more prospects, she could list her on- line but it would take time and the shipping fee would be astronomical. She shuttered at the thought of the huge curly mass traveling across country with her in a sports car. Among other unpleasant problems, the top would need to be down meaning there would be no trunk, no space for luggage.

She opened her purse to get her phone and spotted a small folded strip of paper. It was the one Jay had found in his piece of chocolate at the Well Wishes restaurant, his restaurant.

She started to throw it away but her curiosity won over and she unfolded it and read:

A good woman is hard to find and is worth more than diamonds.

That one wasn't staged. I am not a good woman.

She made an effort not to remember what the note she had received said but remembered the words anyway.

She pulled out her phone and called the local shipping company to have the bed sent.

"I hope I get a call on you soon."

As if in protest, the large dog dug at the bedpost

with her teeth.

"Haven't you done enough damage around here or are you going for total destruction? Get down! Stop it! You are scratching the brass!"

She pulled Prism back, detaching her jaw from the top of the brass post.

"It might not mean much to you, but....

Laven stopped herself wondering why she cared that the dog chewed on the circular end that capped the bedpost. Did the bed now hold sentimental value to her?

The magnifying glass had been stolen and with it went any meaning. Had she moved past the fact that her mother had left her this tarnished piece of furniture and left the house to a complete stranger?

She looked at the other inheritance that returned to chewing on the brass and made her decision.

"No, I'll sell this old bed and find you a new home. Too bad she couldn't have taken both of you with

her.

She gave me nothing meaningful throughout my life and ended the tradition in like manner."

I have only loneliness as my inheritance.

Prism was now clawing and gnawing on the sphere shaped metal.

"What are you doing?"

She pulled at the mass of white fleece, but let go when the dog started to bark and scratch forcefully at the bedpost.

"Look what you've done. The top is loose now!" Laven was attempting to twist it back in place, but Prism's bark rose about 17 decibels and she pounced at the post as if it were alive.

"What's with you?"

Prism licked at the post

"Now I suppose you're trying to buff out the etchings you carved with your teeth."

Prism whined.

"What do you want?"

Prism pushed at the brass ball with her nose.

"Okay, that puts you at the scene of the crime. Nose prints are all over it. The crime is depreciating my inheritance. One inheritance is destroying the other. Nice!"

The ball was loose enough to wobble now. Laven watched as the overgrown poodle nudged it off the post and toppled onto the bed.

"You did it. Now what?" But Prism ignored the brass ball and sniffed at the post.

"What smells so good to you? Did something curl up and die in there?"

Laven peeked inside the hollow post and gasped.

Something was curled up all right. She reached in and pulled out a thick roll of bills.

She was even more flabbergasted to learn the denomination of the bills. It wasn't a roll of ones or twenties, but one hundred dollar bills.

She looked down the pipe that served as a bedpost and saw other such wads, one resting on top of another. She pushed the money back into the post and tightened the brass ball securely on top of the post.

Impulsively, she ran over and locked the bedroom door.

"No one can know about this, Prism."

She wondered who, if anyone, already did know.

Is this why someone wants me either gone or dead?

A warmth reached her heart that came close to creating a tear in her eye. Was this a sign that her mother had thought of her.

Money can't buy love, but the fact that she had planned this out and even provided that it would be shipped to her meant that if nothing else, she had considered her future financial well being.

But, why this secrecy? There is a reason she didn't just have it in her will or hadn't just written me a check.

She wondered how much money was hidden there. She struggled to twist off the other balls and discovered there was four times what she had first seen.

"I'm glad you can't talk, Prism. Your nose prints are all over." As soon as the words were out of her mouth, she remembered that her fingerprints were all over the bundle of bills.

She found the rubber gloves used to clean the shower after one of Prism's emergency visits and reopened the original bedpost. She carefully peeled off the first one hundred dollar bill, replaced the bundle with rubber-covered fingers and re-secured the brass sphere.

"Not a word, Prism. Not one bark!"

Chapter 16

~~~

THE STASH OF CURRENCY may be the catalyst of the threats. No one must learn of this discovery. That shouldn't present much of a problem. She had only the handsome shrink and the frequent visiting men in blue to talk to now. One was a stranger and the other two, if they knew about this, would have rolls of green reasons to keep her here longer.

There remained no reason for her to be detained. She would convince the authorities that she would be available via telephone.

She had to leave this place. Excitement and hope had been crushed by disappointment and despair.

This was nothing new, just one additional chapter to her lonely life.

She had ended her ties to What's His Name. The guilt had lessened about the harsh method in doing so by his cavalier attitude of discarding her like yesterday's news. He had inconsiderately tossed her over to someone else to contend with.

Foolish girl! What would make you think you were worth fighting for? There will be females lining up for his magnetic smile.

That internal voice that had tormented her since childhood came again. "You are nothing. No one wants you. No one ever will."

She swallowed hard and looked at the large dog staring at her.

"I hope I can get rid of you soon so I can make this place history," she said as she tucked the keys into her sweater pocket and closed the dog inside the bedroom.

She headed for the garage to pick up the earthly remains of what once was her mother. The small carved box contained the reason she had come here. Lost was any hope of a forever-longed -for hug or words of endearment.

It was time to fulfill her mother's final wishes and scatter her ashes around the lovely little pond at the rear section of her property.

It was a solemn walk to the park -like setting. She should speak reverent words as she performed the sorrowful duty.

No words came. She hadn't known this person. Laven had received gifts from her through the years, but they had only served as a source of pain. They told her that her mother knew she was there, but didn't love her enough to share in her life.

The small box was difficult to open. Laven removed her sweater and tucked it behind the stone chair. A tree branch completely covered it so she made a mental note not to forget it when she returned to the house.

She unwrapped the plastic bag that held the ashes and spoke aloud.

"Wherever you are, I am fulfilling your wishes. I forgive you for not fulfilling mine. Rest in peace."

Laven fought for sincerity on the forgiveness part of what she said. Maybe her mother hadn't had a mother. She would never know.

A portion of the ashes blew in the wind, so was blown any chance of ever being touched by her much-yearned-for mother. She tightened the plastic around the remaining ashes and sat for a moment of reflection.

The recent rain had coaxed more flowers out of the ground, which couldn't have been timelier than if preordered for the occasion. As the ashes floated down, the rustling leaves danced to the chime of the bamboo stalks. What a perfect place to be the last, Laven thought.

Her gaze rested on the ornamental ironwork fence on the other side of the pond.

It was different today. The gate was open and there was a huge hump of dirt inside with a shovel stuck in it.

Someone must be preparing to plant something.

Curious, Laven sat the plastic sack of remaining ashes on the flat rock. She walked around the pond and stepped inside the fenced area. She stood at the edge of a deep hole. It looked to be a root cellar with a wooden hatch door. A pair of large garden scissors was dangerously stuck in the soft soil with the blades jutting upward.

Laven heard nothing other than the music of the drying foliage, but all at once a powerful shove from behind caused her to stumble forward and fall head first into the open hole.

The sides of the icy, cold blades hit painfully on her forehead forcing the blades down and the handle up and onto her eye. She laid face down trying to figure out what had just happened. The noise of the wooden door slamming shut, a crunching sound, and loose dirt falling, forced her to realize that it was she that was being planted in the fenced garden. She turned herself over.

Dazed and not knowing what to do, she withheld a scream. Only the one covering her with soil would hear it. She pulled out from under her head the large scissors that, but for her tripping on her own foot, would have lunged into her upper body and impaled her.

The person on the ground above was seriously trying to cut her life short. Fear gripped her as she lay silently until she heard no movement from up above.

I've been buried alive. No one knows. No one cares.

Her eye throbbed, but the remainder of her body was numb as she poked at the make shift ceiling with the large scissors left for her. She pushed with her legs but stopped when she realized the door wouldn't budge. The strenuous effort only paid to sink her deeper into the soft soil and caused her to breath heavier.

With every breath I exhale, I am poisoning the air with carbon dioxide. I am going to die of affixation.

She screamed in vain for help. Who could hear her voice gagged by the pile of dirt on top of her? Rustling leaves and chiming bamboo would overcome any sound that might struggle out.

There was no one to help, no one to care. How long would it take for anyone to realize she was missing? Time was not on her side.

Her teeth chattered. Her body trembled. She had come here to scatter her mother's ashes, but did not plan to attend her own burial at the same time. Ironically, they would be achieving, in death, what Laven had hoped for in life. They would be together now.

The earthen, musty smell was so heavy that she could taste dirt. It was hard to swallow, hard to breathe. With every exhalation, she emitted more poison into this small space. She was exchanging oxygen for carbon dioxide.

Time. How long have I been here, fifteen minutes or a year? How much longer can I breathe in my own exhaust?

She decided that the chances of someone coming out here to help her were in the negative range. The thought compelled her to let out more carbon dioxide

One eye pulsated with pain while the other was

wide open. Darkness surrounded her.

Darkness has no speed. It just closes around you and swallows you up.

This is how she would die. Nothing happens when nothing goes away. Nothing minus nothing equals nothing. There would be no loss, no one to mourn her, no one to miss her.

This is the final stage of loneliness.

She remembered Jay warning her not to wait until she was knocked down to reach for God. She thought of his annoying radio station and that song that he said was one of his favorites. The words played in the deafening silence of her mind.

When I can't get up and I can't go on

Cause you are my light in the dark.

When I'm plagued with pain and filled with fear

I run to you and you alone.

When my days are few and death is near

I run to you.

"God!" she screamed. "If You are everywhere, you can hear me. Jay said that You cared for me. If that's true and You are listening, I give what's left of my miserable life to you. Please take me."

Her muscles relaxed and her teeth stopped hitting each other. She lay still on the bed of dirt. A peace blanketed over her.

"I'm dying."

With a power that wasn't her own, she raised her arms. Like a conduit, a warmth flowed down them.

There was an unfamiliar weight that rested in her hands. A feeling, like none that she had experienced before, permeated through her being.

An overwhelming love embraced her. Then tears began to flow from her eyes, tears that had been bottled up for years broke free. She was free.

Laven spoke out loud within the acoustic walls of dirt. "You love me, Lord! You love me like I am Your only child. I am Your little girl and You love me.

You are here with me."

Laven felt a pull and she wanted nothing more than to be with Jesus, to be in His arms.

"I'm ready, God. Please forgive me for not seeking you before. I'm ready to be with You."

An unnatural peace flowed through her. Laven wondered if this peace is what carries a martyr, a person dying for their faith into the loving arms of Jesus. Now she knew that God bestows an overwhelming power on his children in time of deep trouble.

She lowered her arms and closed her eyes. "I'm dying now." And she smiled.

Chapter 17

~~~

FAR AWAY, AN INTENSE commotion was happening. Scrapping and tugging could be heard in the distance. A loud screeching sound and then suddenly a heavy weight was thrust on her followed by moist wet strokes all over her face.

One of Laven's eyes wouldn't open while brightness hit the other. The heavy panting of a very big dog welcomed her.

"I don't like you, Prism." Laven's words were weak. "I Love you!"

Prism barked and twirled her tail while Laven worked to pull herself up.

Weak and sore, she managed out of the horizontal earthen box and glanced back with the eye that wasn't hurting at the large scissors that were intended to spill her blood.

The gate was closed but not locked. Was her attacker planning a return visit?

She hurried around the pond to the rock she had used for a chair and grabbed her sweater hidden behind it. The onyx box and plastic bag containing the remainder of her mother's ashes was gone. She had no time to think about it now.

The poodle and the brand new Laven rushed to the house.

"Prism, I don't have to be alone anymore. God will walk with me through the trials of this life. I no longer fear death. I have had a glimpse to the other side and I saw an unbelievable love there."

A loyal panting sound was the response

Looking at the camera on the eve of the house, she

wondered how long she had been imprisoned in dirt and if it had captured an image of her capturer.

~

Laven stroked Prism's head as she answered questions. This time it was not just the two familiar uniformed policemen; with them was a team of plain-clothed officers searching the house for fingerprints and other things that could be used as evidence.

It felt good to be believed, but the feeling paled drastically to how it felt to truly believe.

She was wrapped in a wool blanket and blanketed in God's love. She convinced the paramedics that there was no need for a trip to the hospital, but gladly accepted an icepack for her eye.

Prism let out a barking alarm and right away, as always, there was a knock at the door. The policeman let in another individual carrying a laptop.

He introduced himself and sat down next to Laven. He opened the computer that showed footage from the security cameras.

"There was a lot of activity in your yard, Ms. Hoddy."

He froze a frame and enlarged the picture.

"Do you know this man?"

Laven looked closely at the image and focused on the dark eyes. It looked like eyeliner.

"He's the man at the airport who rented me the car."

One of the frequent visiting cops stepped forward.

"This looks like the man who hit the car she was driving and then fled the scene."

"Do you know who he is?"

"No, I never saw him prior to renting the car from him."

"What rental company was he with?"

"That has already been checked out. The company was bogus, perhaps a cover," answered the Man in Blue.

Laven pulled toward the computer and watched the moving footage of days prior.

Chills ran up her back to realize there were people in the yard that she was unaware of, people who meant her harm.

Was this what Lula warned her about?

She scratched Prism's shoulder as a silent plea for forgiveness. Laven had scolded her for her persistent barking at times when she was probably giving warnings.

"An older security camera, placed on the side of the house prior to the new ones being installed, captured the frames you are about to view."

She watched as the screen revealed a figure dressed in black, complete with a hoodie and face cover, at the side of the house climbing up and into the window.

"That's the one!"

The operator of the computer froze the frame.

"How can you tell who this is with the face covered?"

"I just know that it's the one who stole my magnifying glass!"

He began the video again.

"Are you rerunning the film?"

"No, this is continuous footage."

Laven watched. It was someone in black again. This time there was no hoodie, just long black stringy hair.

"Look, this time you can see the face. It's a girl."

"Remember the camera didn't stop. This is a second individual."

He froze the frame and enlarged it.

"Do you know her?"

Laven stared at the girl on the screen. She had a piercing through her eyebrow, one in her nose and another in her lower lip. Her eyes were heavily made up. Despite all these distractions, there was something familiar about the facial structure, something that turned Laven's stomach.

"No! It couldn't be."

"Do you know her?"

"It looks like someone I saw at the airport. And I think..."

Laven paused and stared at the picture.

The years had been rough on her; she was sure that the girl had also been rough on the years.

"She might be.."

"Who?"

"Someone from my past."

"Do you have a name?"

"Sally Ella Rue."

The name was hard to roll off of her tongue.

Could it be possible that she continued to be so driven by hate and jealousy that she could be trying to hurt or even kill me after all these years?

The computer footage continued to run.

Her face was so contorted that it appeared evil. Laven slid to the edge of the sofa and watched as the girl poked a thick stick in the window frame to hold it in place while she removed the box of candy. She ripped off the cellophane and stuck it in her pocket.

She opened the white box and stuffed a couple of chocolates in her mouth before she poked a hypodermic needle in the other pieces. She then traded the stick for the box and ran through the fallen leaves and into the lilac bushes.

"Kill!"

"What?"

"She injected the chocolates with poison. She nearly killed this dog."

The film continued to roll.

"Wait, here is someone else walking toward the window."

All at once embarrassment shaded Laven's face. She recognized herself heading for the flower box beneath the kitchen window. An event she hoped to forget was soon to be relived before a live audience.

"That will be me. Can we just replay the previous footage."

"We need to see if we captured anyone who was responsible for burying you in the hole."

The operator was maneuvering the computer when one of the plain clothed officers entered the living room.

"Have you had visitors with red hair?"

Laven thought before she answered. Jay and Lula had been her only visitors, neither of which had red hair.

"No."

"This would say otherwise." He held up a plastic bag containing hair so red she could see it from several feet away.

"Red hair! The vet found red hair in Prism's mouth and under her collar when we took her in after being poisoned."

"Do you know anyone with red hair?"

"No."

~

The hot shower soothed her sore muscles but stung at her abrasions. She was too sore to think about the painful humiliation of sharing scenes of her backside wiggling outside the window on the security film.

She carefully dried herself, slipped into her robe, and wrapped a towel around her head.

She stared at the swollen bluish purple slit where her eye with the golden flecks once resided.

As she rubbed lotion carefully on her tender skin, she recounted her mother's last words. "Magnifying glass , J..."

She started to say Jesus, but must have been called home and finished saying His name in His very presence. She sent for me to tell me about Jesus.

Laven wondered if she would have listened to her advice to make Him her Savior. She hadn't listened to Jay. It took her looking into the eyes of death to submit her will to Him.

I have to tell Jay why my mother sent for me and Who found me.

She wore her new white jacket and sped away in the sports car. There wasn't much time before the cruiser was scheduled to depart the dock for the day.

Just as she came to the last stop light before leaving town, her phone rang.

It must be Jay. He is the only one who has my number.

The caller wasn't Jay.

Laven answered the question posed to her in a decisive manner.

"No. I'm sorry; she is no longer for sale. I have decided to keep her myself."

That furry mess has not only saved my life, she has stolen my heart.

The parking lot was full so she parked in the last row of cars. She was sore, but she had to run as she dug in her purse for the ticket.

She made it just as the ramp was being removed. The large boat was full. She wondered if she should have called to make sure Jay was going on the cruise after their fight. Maybe he decided he did not want to go alone.

She climbed the stairs to the top deck hoping it would give her a better view. The sun sparkled like diamonds on the water. The view of the lake was beautiful, but what she observed on the lower deck gave her pause. There in midst of a crowd of people stood Jay. He had not come alone. A girl with long dark hair had her arms around him and was close enough to give him a kiss. She did.

I'll stay out of sight and not ruin his day.

She stopped herself.

Wait! What I have to tell him will not ruin his day; it will make it.

"Jay!" She called loudly, hoping he could hear her voice over the musicians' soft music and lively conversation of the crowd.

He looked around and finally up. She could see even from that distance his flashing smile. He motioned for her to come down and she immediately accepted his silent invitation.

She worked her way through the crowd and walked up to him. Before she could speak, he addressed her.

"Whoa! You either ran out of eye shadow before you made it to the second eye or someone gave you a whopper of a shiner. I have to hear about that."

Laven looked at the beautiful girl who had kissed him on the cheek and was relieved to find that it wasn't Mercedes. "I don't want to interrupt you, I just.."

The beautiful girl broke in, "No, it's me that is interrupting. Jay has been expecting you."

How could he have been expecting me? I wasn't even expecting me to be here.

It was Jay's turn to talk. "Laven, meet my cousin, Liberty. Neither of us knew the other would be on the day cruise. We haven't seen each other for a while."

Justice and Liberty? Was there another relative named For All? What was it with this family?

"Wait a minute! I know you! You are the nurse I met at the hospital. I didn't recognize you with your hair down."

"That's right! It looks like you have a had a few bumps and bruises since I last saw you."

The two exchanged friendly conversation and then the one who was given the same name as a famous bell walked away.

"What happened to you?" Jay stepped closer to look at her swollen eye.

"Oh, Jay, I have so much to tell you that I don't even know where to begin."

"Always start with what is the most important."

"Okay, I gave my heart to God. I don't just know about Him, I really know Him." Laven felt like she was smiling on the inside.

Jay's face radiated with excitement. "Oh, Laven, I knew it was going to be a struggle for you, but it looks like it was a knock down drag out!"

He doesn't know how accurate that description is!

"Oh, Laven." He said it again only this time, he pulled her close to him.

Laven didn't pull back even though her muscles were sore. In fact, she leaned in a bit and gave him a hug.

They rested in each other's arms for a while and then Laven spoke.

"Now for the second thing I have to tell you. My mother's last words were, Magnifying Glass, J. I believe she was going to say Jesus before He took her to be with Him."

"That's beautiful, Laven."

"I just wish I hadn't lost the magnifying glass. I believe there was more to it, more that she wanted me to know. Otherwise she would have used the extra words to finish His name.

I know it was important, Jay."

Jay spoke softly to her. "I'll do what I can to find it, Laven. If you are supposed to get it back, you will. You now possess the most important thing on this temporal earth and no one can take it away from you."

"God's love?" Laven asked.

Jay nodded and took her hand in his.

She remembered the lifting of her being that she had felt while in the small dirt dungeon. She remembered that intense euphoria she had experienced when God revealed his love for her.

God's love is all I need. It is really all I have ever needed. He was that missing piece in my life. He was the key that unlocked the chains of the past.

The water shifted the boat and a waiter carrying a tray of drinks lost his balance and the liquid in the glasses was transferred on to Laven.

Everything had changed after her close call with death. Everything had been assigned a new value in her life. Her priorities were all being realigned.

"Look." she said playfully. "Free drinks!"

She pointed at her new white coat that was now covered in red stains.

"Care to share?" He played back and pulled her close enough to blot some of the red coloring onto his own clothing.

Their stare into each other's eyes seemed to travel into infinitely.

Their lips touched.

But not for long, Laven's ring tone pulled them back to the finite present. By the time she drew the phone from her purse, it had already gone to voice messaging.

She held it to her ear and her good eye grew wide with shock.

"It was my mother! It was her voice! She said she would call me back."

"Until then, shall we resume?"

"Just as well, Justice Well."

Book 2:

UP CLOSE AND DANGEROUS

Pamela's desire in writing is not only to bring her characters to life, but to point her readers to Life.

Visit : **BeMYBooky.com**

Made in the USA
Monee, IL
20 January 2024

51665826R00166